William—The Explorer

1. Just—William
2. More William
3. William Again
4. William—The Fourth
5. Still—William
6. William—The Conqueror
7. William—The Outlaw
8. William—In Trouble
9. William—The Good
10. William
11. William—The Bad
12. William's Happy Days
13. William's Crowded Hours
14. William—The Pirate
15. William—The Rebel
16. William—The Gangster
17. William—The Detective
18. Sweet William
19. William—The Showman
20. William—The Dictator
21. William and Air Raid Precautions
22. William and the Evacuees
*23. William Does His Bit
*24. William Carries On
*25. William and the Brains Trust
*26. Just William's Luck
27. William—The Bold
28. William and the Tramp
29. William and the Moon Rocket
30. William and the Space Animal
31. William's Television Show

Just—William
a facsimile of the first (1922) edition

The William Companion
by Mary Cadogan

Just William's World – a pictorial
by Gillian Clements and Kenneth

What's Wrong with Civilizashun
by William Brown (and Richmal

D1270092

* A hardback edition of this title is available from
Firecrest Publishing Ltd, Bath, Avon

'YOU WRETCHED BOY!' SCREAMED CYPRIAN. 'YOU'VE RUINED MY
WORKING DAY.'

(*see page 239*)

William—
The Explorer

BY

RICHMAL CROMPTON

Illustrated by Thomas Henry

PAN MACMILLAN
CHILDREN'S BOOKS

First published 1960

© Richmal Crompton Lamburn 1960

Illustrations copyright Thomas Henry Fisher Estate

First published in this edition 1991 by

PAN MACMILLAN CHILDREN'S BOOKS
A division of Pan Macmillan Limited
London and Basingstoke
Associated companies throughout the world

ISBN 0-333-55549 X

A CIP catalogue record for this book is available from the
British Library

Typeset by Macmillan Production Limited
Printed and bound in Great Britain by
Clays Ltd, St Ives plc

Contents

1 WILLIAM—THE EXPLORER 1

2 WILLIAM AND THE NATURE RAMBLE 32

3 JUMBLE FINDS A CAREER 65

4 DON WILLIAM AND THE SUN-BATHER 98

5 WILLIAM AND THE PAYING GUEST 132

6 WILLIAM GETS HIS FAIRING 160

7 WILLIAM AND THE TELEVISION INVENTION 184

8 WILLIAM AND THE FORCE OF HABIT 215

An invitation from William

Join my club and becum a noutlaw

William Brown

You can join the Outlaws Club!
You will receive
✱ a special Outlaws wallet containing
your own Outlaws badge
the Club Rules
and
a letter from William giving you the secret password

To join the Club send a letter with your name and address written in block
capitals telling us you want to join the Outlaws, and a postal order for
45p, to

The Outlaws Club
Children's Marketing Department
18–21 Cavaye Place
London SW10 9PG

You must live in the United Kingdom or the Republic of Ireland in order
to join.

Chapter 1

William—The Explorer

'Well, we've got to *do* somethin' about it,' said William. 'It'll prob'ly go as quick as it came an' we'll feel jolly fed up if we haven't *done* somethin' about it.'

The Outlaws had awakened that morning to find the countryside covered by a heavy fall of snow – familiar tracts obliterated; gardens, roads and fields one white unbroken tract that shimmered in the wintry sunshine. They had assembled at William's gate, ready for any activity that William's fertile brain might devise. Henry had arrived panting a few minutes after the others.

'She made me sweep the snow away from the front path before I came out,' he explained. ('She', in Henry's vocabulary, always meant his mother.)

'That's all they think of doin' with it, sweepin' it away,' said William in a tone of disgust. 'It *spoils* it, sweepin' it away. Gosh, it might never have come at all if they start sweepin' it away the minute it comes. They jus' don't deserve it, the way they mess about with it.'

'Well, what'll we *do*?' said Ginger impatiently.

'We've gotter *think*,' said William, and his brows knit themselves together in the complicated pattern that always accompanied his moments of deep thought.

'Snowball fight,' suggested Ginger.

1

'Gosh, no!' said William contemptuously. 'It's kids' stuff, snowball fights.'

'We might make a snowman,' suggested Douglas, but the glance that William threw him disposed of the suggestion without words.

'We've got to do somethin' we've never done before,' said William. His brow cleared and a light broke over his countenance. '*Tell* you what! Winter sports! It's a jolly good idea. We've never done winter sports. That's what we'll do. We'll do winter sports.'

The others considered the suggestion with interest.

'What do they do in them?' said Ginger.

'They toboggan an' ski an' skate an' all sorts of things.'

'Our toboggan's come to pieces an' we haven't any skis or skates,' said Henry.

'Well, we can get 'em, can't we?' said William irritably. 'The minute I s'gest anythin' you start makin' objections. People *get* 'em, don't they? They aren't *born* wearing 'em, are they?' His voice took on its note of heavy sarcasm as he continued, 'Well, it's news to *me* if people are born wearin' skis an' skates an' toboggans.'

'My father's got an alpenstock,' said Douglas. 'It's a sort of walkin' stick for climbin' mountains with.'

'Well, you can borrow that,' said William.

'He might not lend it me,' said Douglas.

'No, he prob'ly wouldn't,' said William. 'I didn't say he'd lend it to you. I said you could borrow it. An' we could tie that ole toboggan together with string.'

'That leaves skis an' skates,' said Ginger.

'Robert's got some ski boots an' Ethel's got some skates,' said William.

'An' I bet they've got them put away somewhere

where *you* can't get at 'em,' said Henry with a short laugh.

'Yes, they prob'ly have,' admitted William, 'but I can have a jolly good look for 'em. I bet they won't notice if I do find 'em, too. They can't think of anythin' else but this ole lecture an' this ole dance.'

It happened that an Under Thirty Club had been formed in the village and Robert had been elected President. Robert took his duties seriously. Each Saturday he arranged a function for the members, interspersing the purely social with the elevating and instructive. On one Saturday he would have a dance and on the next a lecture or discussion. Last Saturday they had had a dance. Next Saturday they were to have a lecture on 'Living Marvels' by a famous entomologist.

Ethel, who was a member of the club, had a way of evading the more improving fixtures and had accepted for this Saturday an invitation to Peggy Barlow's birthday party, which was to take the form of a fancy dress dance. It was unfortunate that the two dates should coincide, but the entomologist had chosen his date before Peggy Barlow had decided to have her party and neither could be changed. The Under Thirty Club had dealt with the situation in a realistic fashion. The more earnest-minded were going to the lecture, the less earnest-minded to the dance. The Under Thirties were more or less equally divided into the two camps and both functions – one to be held in the Church Room, the other in the Village Hall – would be adequately attended. William felt only scorn for the dance, but the title 'Living Marvels' roused his interest.

'Is he going to talk about that monster that lived in a lock somewhere?' he asked Robert.

'The Loch Ness Monster?' said Robert. 'No. Don't be so ridiculous. Of course he isn't. Anyway, the creature's mythical.'

'Well, it may be,' said William non-committally. 'I don't know anythin' about that. But it's *real*, 'cause I read about it once in a newspaper an' it was written by someone that had axshully *seen* it . . . Anyway, if you're not goin' to have him, why not have a Sea Serpent? I met a sailor at the seaside once that'd *seen* one. He said it was ten feet long an' had horns. If this lecturer could get a photo of one—'

'Don't talk such nonsense,' snapped Robert. He was trying to write a letter to the lecturer, confirming the arrangements and telling him that the Vicar offered him hospitality for the night. Already, distracted by William's questions, he had put too many l's in 'hospitality' and too few m's in 'committee'. 'I wish you'd go away.'

'Well, listen,' said William. 'If he's not goin' to talk about the Loch Ness Monster or the Sea Serpent, what about the 'Bominable Snowman? I bet he'll talk about that.'

'Of course he won't. That doesn't exist, either,' said Robert.'

'Not *exist*!' said William. 'Gosh! You don't know what you're talkin' about. The 'Bominable Snowman? *'Course* it exists. Why, it's been on the pictures. It *mus'* be real.'

'Oh, shut up!' said Robert.

'What *is* he goin' to talk about, then?'

'Oh, ants and bees and spiders and things,' said Robert, running his fingers wildly through his hair. He had now left an 'r' out of 'arrangements' and almost written 'Snowman' instead of 'Living Marvels'.

'Jus' insects!' said William scornfully. 'Gosh! There's nothin' to insects. I've kept 'em myself. I kept a spider in a jam jar for a fortnight once an' it didn't do anythin' but sit about an' look bored. I don't call *that* int'restin'. I don't call *that* a livin' marvel. I—'

'Will – you – go – away!' said Robert between clenched teeth.

William went away.

And in the night had come the fall of snow that had driven everything else out of his mind.

'Where shall we do these winter sports?' said Henry.

'Well, we want a hill,' said William. 'You have to have a hill for skis an' toboggans.'

'There's a hill on the road to Marleigh,' said Ginger.

'We'll try that,' said William.

They tried it, but it was not a success. The road was a main road, much frequented by buses, motors, cycles and vans. After undergoing several hairbreadth escapes and receiving streams of abuse from infuriated drivers, they decided to abandon the project.

'It's jus' what my father was sayin' the other day,' said William sternly. 'Drivers seem to've lost all sense of responsibility. The roads jus' aren't safe for pedestrians nowadays. An' they've messed up all the snow. There isn't enough left to do winter sports on. Let's go on to Marleigh an' see if we can find a good hill there.'

Accompanied by Jumble, who had played his full part in the hairbreadth escapes, they made their way to Marleigh, and there they found the ideal hill. It was a field that sloped down sharply behind a small square house called Hill View, ending in a long flat run. The field was enclosed by a hedge, but hedges presented no great difficulty to the Outlaws. Their small but solid forms could worm their way through hedges with incredible rapidity, leaving, after several passages, a serviceable hole for future use.

They had repaired the toboggan as best they could by tying it together with string and it gave them a brief but hilarious descent before it came to pieces. They mended it and tried again, using Douglas's father's alpenstock to guide it on its way. The descent was briefer and more hilarious. Tiring eventually of this, they put on Robert's ski boots, fastening flat pieces of wood for skis, and skied down the slope in turn, ending up in a confusion of skis and skiers – a confusion made worse confounded by Jumble, who ran round them in frenzied circles, tripping them up and chasing their skis through the snow.

But a thaw was already setting in. Melted snow was dropping from trees and hedges.

'We'll come back quick after lunch,' said William breathlessly as they collected what was left of their sports equipment at the end of the morning. 'Gosh! It may be all gone if we don't hurry.'

In a businesslike and hasty fashion, he swallowed down generous helpings of toad-in-the-hole and apple pie for lunch, then hurried off to meet the others. Henry held a half-eaten piece of treacle tart in his hand, Ginger was still munching his last mouthful of jam roly-poly and Douglas had thrust a slab of marmalade pudding into his pocket, where it was now inextricably mixed with other occupants – string, biscuit crumbs, sherbet, ants' eggs, pistol caps and marbles.

Led by William, they ran across the fields to Marleigh and scrambled through the hedge. The field, still snow-covered, presented a curious surface of concentric and eccentric circles, marking the scene of their morning's activities. But William's attention had strayed to the fence that enclosed the garden of Hill View. There was evidently a shed, built against the fence inside the garden, whose sloping roof was covered by about eight inches of snow.

'Look!' he said. 'I bet we could make an avalanche of that. It's jolly loose. If we jus' gave it a shove . . . Come on. Let's try.'

They climbed the fence and surveyed the empty garden.

'No one's there,' said William. 'Come on. Let's give it a shove.'

Using the pieces of stick that had served as their skis, they gently edged the block of snow forward. The result surpassed their highest expectations. Slowly, smoothly, moving in one mass, the wedge of snow slid down the roof of the shed, and collapsed upon the path beneath.

And from the mass of fallen snow there rose a bellow – a bellow strangled by the avalanche but none the less eloquent of rage and anguish.

For it happened that Mr Jones, the owner of Hill View, had gone into his shed to make sure that his dahlia tubers were sufficiently protected against the frost and, on emerging from the shed, had received the full impact of William's avalanche.

'Gosh!' said William as he scrambled down. 'Let's get off quick.'

But they were too late. Already Mr Jones had appeared at the little gate that separated the garden from the field and was hailing them with a loud and peremptory shout. They stood, a small apprehensive group, hung about with the sports equipment that they had hastily gathered together, awaiting him.

Mr Jones was a short man and his recent encounter with the avalanche had given him the appearance of a disintegrating snowman, but there was a portentous dignity about him as he strode across the field to confront the culprits.

'How *dare* you!' he sputtered, shaking snow from his head and nose and ears. 'How *dare* you play this outrageous trick on me! How—'

Rage choked him so that he could say no more.

'But listen,' protested William. 'It was an accident. We didn't know you were there. Listen! We didn't know you were there. We're sorry. It was an avalanche an' we didn't know you were there. It was an accident an' an avalanche an' we didn't know you were there an' we're sorry.'

But Mr Jones's eyes had turned to the field – to the whorls and gyrations that were traced in the snow.

'Is that *your* work?' he said. 'Have you had the audacity, the effrontery, to trespass on my private property?'

'We didn't know,' said William. 'We didn't know it was your prop'ty. We've not done it any harm. We've only disarranged the snow a bit. We'll put it straight for you if you like.'

'Be off with you!' said Mr Jones savagely. Melted snow was trickling down his spine. 'If you as much as set foot in the place again, I'll send for the police. Be off with you!'

The Outlaws retreated as quickly as possible, dragging their sports equipment with them, followed by Jumble, who turned as soon as he was on the safe side of the hedge to bark defiance at the enemy.

Mr Jones stood and watched them, his small face

twisted into an expression of agony as another stream of melted snow made its way slowly down his spine.

It was not only William's avalanche that had upset Mr Jones; he had been feeling upset even before he went into the shed to look at his dahlia tubers. In fact he had only gone into the shed to look at his dahlia tubers in order to take his mind off his other troubles. It was Mr Jones's father who had upset Mr Jones. Mr Jones's father was an old gentleman of 79 – as carefree and irresponsible as his son was sober and responsible.

Mr Jones was an old friend of the Barlows and had been invited to Peggy's fancy dress dance. He had unwisely mentioned the fact in a letter to his father, adding that he naturally did not intend to accept the invitation. And by return of post he had received a letter from his father saying that he would come to spend the week-end with his son and that they would go to the fancy dress dance together. Mr Jones's father loved parties and he loved fancy dress dance parties above all others. He was bringing two costumes – the Mock Turtle, which he would wear, and the Mad Hatter, which his son would wear. He would arrive early on Saturday with the two costumes and intended to enjoy every minute of the festivities.

Mr Jones was fond of his father. He looked on him as an indulgent parent might look on a high-spirited tempestuous child. But whereas even an indulgent parent can, when put to it, generally control his child, Mr Jones could not control his father. His protests and remonstrances only amused the old man.

'You're a stick-in-the-mud, my dear Aloysius,' he would say. 'If I didn't come down to jerk you out of your rut every now and then, you'd turn into a regular fossil.'

And, whenever Mr Jones thought of Saturday and imagined himself decked out in the ignominious costume of the Mad Hatter, everything in him seemed to curl up into a tight little ball of shame and misery. He would never, he thought, live the thing down. Never, for the rest of his life, would anyone see him without remembering his appearance in that idiotic costume. And the most humiliating part of it all was that Aloysius's slightly prominent nose and slightly retreating chin gave him a faint – a very faint – resemblance to the Mad Hatter of Tenniel's illustrations. Desperately he sought ways of escape, though he knew that the old man would ride roughshod, with careless good humour, over all his objections. For, when the old man was set on a thing, nothing had ever been known to stop him.

'Do you good, my boy,' he would say. 'Take you out of your rut.'

And Mr Jones pictured himself in the appalling check suit, the outrageous spotted tie, the preposterous hat – an object of ridicule to the whole neighbourhood. The old man, of course, would be the success of the evening, bouncing happily about in his Mock Turtle costume, but Aloysius would drink his cup of humiliation to its dregs. It had been a relief to turn his anger on to the wretched boys who had doused him in snow and run riot in his field.

'Hooliganism!' he muttered as he returned to the house. 'Rank hooliganism! Unpardonable! Scandalous! Shocking!'

He whipped up his anger against the trespassers because only by so doing could he keep his thoughts away from the horrors of Peggy Barlow's party and his Mad Hatter's costume.

'Gosh! Wasn't he in a bate!' said William, as the four made their way homeward. 'All that fuss jus' for a bit of snow! Gosh! People've been *buried* in the snow an' had to be dug out by dogs without makin' all that fuss. Why, people've been *killed* by snow before now. He's lucky, when you come to think of it, jus' gettin' a bit on his head. He ought to be *grateful*.'

'I dunno about that,' said Ginger doubtfully, impressed, as usual, by William's eloquence but suspecting a weak spot in the logic.

'We can't do any more winter sports there now,' said Henry.

'Well, it's starting to thaw, anyway,' said Douglas, 'an' the snow'll be gone by the mornin', so it doesn't matter.'

But the snow had not gone by the morning. The thaw had stopped in the night and by the morning snow was again falling heavily.

It was the day of the lecture and the party. Robert hurried from home to lecture-room, from lecture-room to home, arranging chairs, putting 'reserved' notices on the front row, filching a table-cloth and a vase of flowers from his mother's sitting-room to adorn the speaker's table on the platform, wrestling with an antiquated and temperamental heating stove that, on its bad days (and today was evidently one of them), hiccuped loudly at regular intervals and belched forth clouds of black smoke. Hurrying to and fro, stern-browed and eagle-eyed, he was composing, with ever-increasing nervousness, the speech in which, as President, he was to introduce the speaker.

William watched him morosely.

'Insects!' he muttered. 'Jus' ordin'ry insects, when he could talk about the 'Bominable Snowman!'

'Oh, shut up!' said Robert and continued under his breath: ' . . . no need to introduce such a distinguished scientist . . . such a distinguished scientist needs no introduction from me . . . it would be an impertinence on my part to attempt to introduce such a distinguished scientist . . .'

'I bet it's not too late to stop him talkin' about insects,' said William. 'Jus' tell him when he comes he's got to change his lecture round to the 'Bominable Snowman.'

' . . . a pleasure and a privilege to welcome such a distinguished scientist,' muttered Robert, then, raising his voice to a bellow, 'Get – out – of – my – way.'

William got out of his way.

Ethel, who had originally decided to go to the fancy dress dance as 'Sweet Lavender' from the 'Old Cries of London', had changed her mind at the last minute and decided to go as 'Cherry Ripe'. She was now up in her bedroom, stitching bunches of artificial cherries on to every available point of her costume.

Mrs Brown, who was helping Mrs Barlow with the refreshments, had shut herself into the kitchen, her mental horizon bounded on all sides by pastries and patties and soufflés and creams.

Mr Brown was away in the North on business.

A pleasant feeling of assurance crept over William that, for this day at any rate, he would be left pretty much to his own devices.

Mrs Brown sent him into Hadley in the morning to collect some biscuits and *petits fours* that had been ordered at the confectioner's, and Robert collared him after lunch and sent him into Hadley again to buy a tin of widely advertised chemical compound that, he hoped, would pacify the stove.

So it was not till late afternoon that William could set off to join the Outlaws.

Standing at Ginger's gate, they saw him plodding towards them, dragging the dilapidated sledge, its contents covered by his Red Indian tent, with Jumble, frisking exuberantly through the snow, at his side. He wore Wellington boots, a raincoat, a beret of Robert's and a brightly coloured woollen scarf of Ethel's wound tightly about his neck.

'You've been a jolly long time comin',' said Henry reproachfully.

'Yes, I had to help 'em with this dance an' lecture,' said William nonchalantly. 'Seems sometimes as if they couldn't do anythin' without me.'

'What are we goin' to do?' said Ginger.

'An Antarctic expedition,' said William. 'It's jus' the day for an Antarctic expedition. Look! I've got everything. I've brought a tent for us to camp in an' provisions.' He drew back the tent from the sledge, revealing a heap of sandwich crusts, a few odds and ends of pastry, some broken biscuits salvaged from his shopping expedition, blobs of cheese, sardine and uncooked cake mixture, quarter of a stale loaf, and a generous supply of cold potatoes and cabbage. 'They're jolly good provisions, an' – look!' He took out a tin that was half buried in cold potatoes and opened it. It contained rice grains. 'That's dehydrated rice pudding. You've got to have dehydrated food on an Antarctic expedition. You mix it with water an' it turns into a rice pudding. We'll mix it with snow an' I bet it'll turn into a *jolly* good rice pudding. An' Jumble's goin' to be the husky an' draw the sledge. You've got to have rubber boots an scarves an' things.' He inspected them with approval. 'Yes, you've got all those.'

Douglas surveyed the darkening landscape, over which the snow was blowing in gusts.

'We're goin' to get caught in an awful storm,' he said.

' 'Course we are,' said William. 'We're not scared of that. Gosh! We'd be jolly funny Antarctic explorers to be scared of a snowstorm. Come on! Let's harness Jumble to the sledge.'

Jumble, who had never really taken to his career as a husky, leapt out of reach, dodging nimbly around the group till he was finally captured by William and attached to the sledge by means of Mrs Brown's clothes-line, which William had thoughtfully brought with him. Harnessed, he sat down in the snow and only after the bribe of a couple of sandwich crusts could be persuaded to apply himself to his duties.

'He's startin' eatin' our provisions already,' said Douglas. 'I've never known him be a husky without eatin' all our provisions.'

'Well, he's got to keep his strength up, hasn't he?' said William indignantly, 'an' they've got to be fed well to keep their strength up. A good explorer'd sooner starve himself than his husky. Gosh! It'd be a nice thing if he started dyin' of hunger before we'd got to our first camp.'

'He doesn't look like doin' that,' said Douglas, watching Jumble, who was hurling himself from side to side in a vain attempt to free himself from his harness.

But at last the procession got under way and began to straggle across the fields. Henry led it, walking backwards and holding out a sheaf of sandwich crusts towards Jumble. Next came Jumble, straining after the dainties,

WILLIAM PLODDED ALONG, WITH JUMBLE FRISKING EXUBERANTLY
AT HIS SIDE.

with Ginger keeping a steadying hand on his collar. Next
came the laden sledge and behind it William, pushing it
along, for Jumble, whenever he felt the weight of the
sledge resting on his shoulders, would hold up proceedings by turning round to growl at it. Last came Douglas,
picking up the odds and ends that fell from the sledge as it
made its erratic progress over the snow.

'It'd be less trouble doin' it without him,' said Ginger
mildly, as he bent down to counter a sudden sideways
lurch of Jumble's.

' 'Course it wouldn't,' said William. 'It wouldn't be an
Antarctic expedition without a husky to pull the sledge.'

'It's you pushin' it,' said Ginger, 'not him pullin' it.'

'Well, he's got to keep his strength up, hasn't he?' said William. 'He's bein' a husky, anyway, an' a jolly good one.'

At this point Henry tripped over a hidden stone and sat down heavily, and Jumble, seizing his opportunity, snatched the remaining sandwich crusts from his hand and swallowed them in one large gulp.

'More of our provisions gone,' said Douglas bitterly. 'We'll be lucky if we've got even the dehydrated rice pudding left by the time he's finished.'

'All right. Let's have a bit ourselves, then,' said William, removing the tent cover of the sledge. 'Jus' a bit. We've got to ration it out, you know.'

They surrounded the sledge and in a few minutes had disposed of everything except the dehydrated rice pudding and some cold cabbage.

'That was jolly good,' said Douglas.

'Yes, but I dunno that we ought to've eaten it all up like this as soon as we've started out,' said William doubtfully. 'I don't think they do in real Antarctic expeditions.'

'We'll we've got to keep our strength up, same as Jumble,' said Ginger.

The procession reformed and continued its way over the fields. The violence of the blizzard was increasing. It swirled round them in a grey mist cutting into their faces, obliterating sky and trees and hedges, giving to the once well-known landscape a strange and unfamiliar air. They trudged on through the stinging grey mist. The daylight was fading and the general greyness was merging into dusk. Their feet sank deeply into the snow at each step, and they had to brace themselves against the biting wind. It occurred to none of them to suggest turning back. To

William, in particular, ordinary life had ceased to exist. He was the leader of an Antarctic expedition. Around him stretched the vast untrodden wastes of the Polar regions. At the end of the day they would pitch their first camp. Next day they would journey on over the unbroken expanse of snow, battling through wind and driving sleet.

But, though ordinary life had ceased to exist for him, a far-away memory came back to him from the past.

'Sayin' there wasn't a 'Bominable Snowman!' he said. ''Course there is! An' I bet this is the sort of day he comes out on, too. I bet we find his footmarks any minute now.'

Suddenly he stopped and gave a gasp.

'Look!' he said.

Their eyes turned to where he was pointing. There, in the snow, were curious animal-like footmarks.

'Gosh!' he said faintly. 'They're his. They mus' be his. The 'Bominable Snowman's. They're not yuman, anyway. They *mus'* be his. Come on! Let's follow them an' see if we can find him.'

The footmarks led them over the field into a small wood that skirted it, and there they seemed to stop.

'He's not here,' said William, looking round.

And suddenly they saw him, stumbling through the bushes. They gave a shout and the strange figure turned. Though snow-encrusted, its face – inhuman, animal-like – was plainly visible. Its arms were curious flapper-like appendages. Its feet ended in the hooves of which the Outlaws had seen the marks in the snow. Its body was brown and sagging and shapeless. It stood there, its flappers dangling, its head turned in their direction.

'It's *him*!' gasped William. 'It's the 'Bominable Snowman!'

'IT'S HIM!' GASPED WILLIAM. 'IT'S THE 'BOMINABLE SNOWMAN!'

* * *

Mr Aloysius Jones's worst fears had been justified. His father had arrived in his liveliest mood. He had brought the two costumes with him, and his rosy wrinkled face was alight with happy anticipation.

'Believe it or not, my boy,' he said, 'I can still dance till the early hours of the morning.'

Aloysius believed it. He gave a strained unhappy smile and looked out of the window at the falling snow.

'I don't really think we can go in this, you know, Father,' he said.

But he said it without much hope.

'Nonsense, my boy!' said Mr Jones, throwing a careless glance out of the window. 'Nonsense! A few flakes of snow never did anyone any harm. Believe it or not, when I was a young man, I walked fifteen miles through weather much worse than this to a dance.'

Again Aloysius believed it. He looked helplessly at the old man.

'But the roads may be completely blocked,' he said. 'It's been snowing all day.'

'Blocked!' echoed the old man. 'Of course they won't be blocked. There's always plenty of traffic along roads. Traffic always keeps the roads clear. And now let's get into our costumes.' He rubbed his hands. His eyes twinkled merrily. 'I'm looking forward to this, you know. I've not been to a fancy dress dance for over a year. And I've not been to a dance at all for nearly four months. Come on, my boy, come on!'

Aloysius gave an unconvincing cough.

'I don't know that I ought to turn out tonight, Father,' he said plaintively. 'I feel I've ·got the beginnings of a cold.' He sank his voice to a low grating note. 'Don't you hear that I'm a little hoarse?'

'A little donkey, you mean,' said the old man with a cackle of laughter. 'Anyway, there's no cure for a cold like a party. I've proved it over and over again. Come on, my boy. Come on!'

Aloysius trailed miserably upstairs to put on the Mad Hatter's costume – the appalling check suit, the outrageous spotted tie, the preposterous hat . . .

When he came down his father was waiting in the hall, dressed in his Mock Turtle costume. His voice boomed zestfully through the mouth opening.

'Look, my boy. I've got you a cup and a sandwich. Makes the job complete, doesn't it.'

'Yes,' said Aloysius, throwing a hunted glance at the

cup and sandwich that stood on the hall chest. 'Yes, yes, yes.'

'Well, come along. Time we started. We don't want to miss anything. I hope they'll have some of the new dances. I've been taking lessons in them. But, all the same, my boy, there's nothing like the Lancers. A grand dance, the Lancers. "Ladies to the centre", tra-la-la.' He hummed the tune and started to the door. 'Well, come along.'

Aloysius was drawing his overcoat over his costume with a certain sense of relief. At least he couldn't see the wretched thing now.

'You're going to put your overcoat on, surely Father?' he said as he saw the old man opening the front door.

'Of course not,' boomed the old man. 'Shouldn't dream of it. Anyway I couldn't get my flappers through the sleeves. And who wants to wear an overcoat for a short drive in a car? Too soft, you young people. Much too soft. Don't forget your cup and sandwich.'

Miserably Aloysius crept out with his cup and sandwich, deposited them at the back of the car, then took his position at the steering wheel.

They set off through the swirling mist.

'It really isn't fit to go out in, Father,' wailed Aloysius. 'It really *isn't*.'

'Nonsense!' said the old man jovially. 'Never knew anyone make such a fuss about a few flakes of snow. It was high time I came to jerk you out of your rut, my boy. I ought to come more often.'

Aloysius made an unhappy bleating sound and drove out of the drive into the lane. Slowly and carefully, peering through the windscreen at the grey sweep of desolation around him, he drove down the lane, across a main road and into another lane. The snow seemed thicker here, but manfully he drove on. The windscreen wiper gave up the struggle but Aloysius drove on doggedly without it. And then the car came to rest on a thicker, higher snowdrift than any of the others and refused to move further.

'What's happened?' said the old man.

'I've got stuck in a drift,' said Aloysius.

'How careless of you, my boy!' said the old man.

'I never thought much of you as a driver, but I hardly expected you to pack up on such a short journey as this. Can't you go on at all?'

'No,' said Aloysius.

'*Surely* you can!'

'No, no, no, no, *no*! It's quite impossible. Look! The snow's nearly up to the wings.'

'We'll walk, then,' said the old man carelessly.

'Of course we can't walk, Father,' said Aloysius. 'There's a garage at the end of the lane. I'll go and see if they can do anything.'

'My dear boy, the Village Hall is only across that field,' said the old man, waving a flapper vaguely over the waste of snow. 'I may be in my 80th year, but my sense of direction is unimpaired. I remember the lie of the land perfectly. About five minutes' walk across the field will bring us to it.'

'It won't, Father,' said Aloysius. 'You stay here and I'll go and find the garage.'

And Aloysius set off, a small heroic figure, battling his way through the driving snowstorm, soon lost in the encroaching mist.

But the old man's obstinacy was aroused. Of course the

Village Hall was just across the field. That boy of his thought he knew everything. He needed teaching a lesson. And suddenly the old man decided to teach him a lesson. He'd get out of the car, make his way across the field and be at the Village Hall by the time Aloysius arrived there.

'I came by the short cut, my boy,' he would say casually. 'I told you about it, but you wouldn't listen.'

He got out of the car, clambered over the snow-heaped stile and began to make his way across the field. He went on and on. There seemed to be no end to the field, no distinguishing features in the landscape at all. He was convinced that he would soon come to the road in which the Village Hall was situated, but he didn't. He peered around him through his eye-holes. The flakes of snow seemed now to be larger, thicker, swirled into fantastic patterns by the wind before they settled on the ground. But he *knew* he was on the right track. He was *sure* he was on the right track. He went on and on and on. There didn't seem to be any road, but there *must* be a road. He was still convinced that in another minute he would reach the road and that the roof of the Village Hall would loom up suddenly before him.

And then he fell into a specially deep drift and, when he had dragged himself out of it, his headpiece had somehow got displaced and he could no longer see out of the eye-holes. He tried to straighten it with his flappers but only made it worse. He remembered that a zip fastener ran up the back of the head. He tried to find it but couldn't. Finally he gave up the attempt and plodded blindly on . . . falling into the snow, picking himself up, falling again . . . His straggling progress seemed to lead him into a sort of wood. He kept banging into trees. And then, when he felt he could go on no longer, he heard voices – muffled, indistinct voices, for his ears were crumpled up inside his headpiece, but certainly voices.

Cautiously the Outlaws approached him.

'Gosh! *Look* at him!' gasped William again. 'The 'Bominable Snowman! An' Robert said there wasn't one. *Gosh!* I wish he could see it.'

'Are they savage?' said Douglas, backing away apprehensively.

' 'Course not,' said William, laying a friendly hand on the gesticulating flapper. 'I b'lieve he's pleased to see us. P'raps he's heard about yumans same as we've heard about him an' I bet his brother told him they didn't exist same as mine did me an' he's jolly glad to find some . . . Look! Jumble likes him.'

For Jumble was fraternising with the stranger, jumping up at him and barking a welcome.

'He mus' be all right if Jumble likes him,' said William, who cherished a touching – and seldom justified – faith in Jumble's powers as a judge of character.

'He's tryin' to talk,' said Henry.

The old man's spirit's had risen. He could not hear what these people were saying, but if he could get them to undo his zip for him he could free his head and at least see where he was.

'Zip!' he shouted.

They gathered round to listen.

'Zip!' shouted the old man again.

'It mus' be his language,' said William. 'It prob'ly means "Hello!" Let's say it back.'

'Zip!' shouted the Outlaws together.

'Zip!' shouted the old man again.

'Zip!' answered the Outlaws.

'Zip!' yelled the old man.

'Well, we can't go on sayin' "Zip!" to him all night,' said William. 'Wonder why he keeps on sayin' it.'

'P'raps it doesn't mean "Hello!" ' said Henry.

'P'raps it's his name,' said Ginger.

'ZIP!' SHOUTED THE OUTLAWS, ALL TOGETHER.

'Yes, I bet that's it,' said William. 'He's tryin' to tell us his name.' He patted the snow-covered shoulder. 'Good ole Zip!' he said reassuringly. 'Good ole Zip!'

The old man succumbed to silent despair.

'Well, what are we goin' to do with him?' said Ginger. 'Pity we can't take his photo jus' to *prove* that he's real. I bet he'll be goin' back into the snow in a minute.'

'*Tell* you what!' said William. 'We'll take him to this ole lecture that Robert's gettin' up. This 'Livin' Marvels' lecture. Gosh! It'll make 'em sit up. They'll be expectin' a lot of silly stuff about insects an' they'll get a real live 'Bominable Snowman. That ole lecturer'll have somethin' to talk *about* now. He'll have somethin' that really *is* a livin' marvel. Come on . . . Come on, Zip . . . Come on, Zip, ole man.'

'It'll be a valuable contribution to science,' said Henry.

They took his flappers and led him gently over the fields towards the village. They manoeuvred him over the stile to the village street, and led him down the village street to the Village Hall. William pushed open the door, then stood, open-mouthed with amazement, gazing about him.

He had come to the wrong place. So constantly had Robert and Ethel talked about the dance and the lecture, the Church Room and the Village Hall, that he'd got them muddled. This room was full of pierrots and pierrettes, of columbines and harlequins, of Napoleons and Boadiceas and Old Mother Hubbards and Hamlets.

And Mr Aloysius Jones was there, his face wearing an expression of almost desperate anxiety.

'Father!' he cried and pulled down the zip at the back of the Mock Turtle's head.

WILLIAM STOOD OPEN-MOUTHED WITH AMAZEMENT. HE HAD COME
TO THE WRONG PLACE.

The old man's head emerged. He looked round
dazedly.

'What on earth happened?' said Aloysius. 'I went back
to the car and found you'd gone. I made my way here and
you weren't here and – we've all been terribly distressed.
The Vicar's set out with one search-party and I was just
going to set out with another. Whatever happened?'

William gazed at them morosely. Disappointment seethed in his heart. He hadn't made a valuable contribution to science. He hadn't discovered the long sought-for 'Bominable Snowman and given the lecturer on 'Living Marvels' something worthy of his title. He'd only found a silly old man in fancy dress who'd got lost in the snow.

'Oh, I just went for a little walk,' said Mr Jones. He had quickly recovered his aplomb. He had, in fact, almost forgotten those moments of despair when he had plodded blindly on through the storm, his feet, in their cumbersome hoof-like coverings, sinking more deeply into the snow at each step. 'I just went for a little walk to while away the time. I admit that I lost my bearings somewhat, but these boys' – he waved a flapper at the Outlaws – 'found and rescued me. So kind and thoughtful of them, wasn't it?'

Aloysius blinked at the Outlaws.

'Yes,' he said. 'Yes, yes, yes.'

Ethel flitted by on the arm of an erratically cushioned Falstaff. She stopped to stare at the Outlaws while Falstaff seized the opportunity to prod his cushion into place.

'What on earth are you doing here?' she said.

Mr Jones hastened to explain.

'I got lost in the snow,' he said. He was beginning to feel a certain pride in his exploit. 'Various search-parties were sent out for me, but these boys, hearing, I suppose, what had happened, made up a search-party of their own and came to look for me. They even brought their dog' – he smiled down at Jumble who was scratching his ear in a slightly puzzled fashion – 'to help in the search, though'

– he gave a cackle of laughter – 'I failed to notice the appropriate little keg of brandy attached to his collar.'

People swarmed round the four boys, congratulating them. Someone had the bright idea of leading them to the buffet at the end of the room where, throwing aside their depression and bewilderment, they set to work zestfully on the piles of sandwiches, patties, jellies and creams that were arranged on the table.

Mrs Brown came along with a dish of *marrons glacés*. She threw William a glance of mild surprise.

'Aren't you in bed, dear?' she said.

'No,' replied William simply.

Then Mrs Barlow called her to help deal with a patent coffee machine that showed signs of exploding and she hurried away.

Mr Jones, too, had thrown aside thoughts of everything but the pleasures of the evening.

'Come along! Come along! Off with your overcoat, Aloysius! You mustn't keep that on now.'

Reluctantly Aloysius shed his overcoat and stood cringing and cowering in the full shame of his Mad Hatter's costume. A gust of laughter went up in which he read ridicule and contempt. He blinked distractedly.

'But you can't go on wearing that Mock Turtle costume, dear Mr Jones,' Mrs Barlow was saying. 'It's simply soaked.'

The old man looked down at his sodden costume. His rosy face clouded over.

'I suppose I can't,' he said.

He looked wistfully at his son. A wild hope leapt in Aloysius's breast.

'Would you like this costume, Father?' he said.

'Don't you mind?' said the old man humbly. 'Don't you really mind? It seems so mean to take yours. Well, if you *really* don't mind . . . I couldn't bear to be at a fancy dress dance without a fancy dress and of course this one is certainly unwearable. But how shall we change and what will you wear?'

And here Mrs Merton could help them. She lived next door. Her husband was just about the same size as Aloysius. He would lend him a suit. She swept them off with her. In a remarkably short time they returned, Mr Jones Senior gay and debonair as the Mad Hatter, his son dignified and correct in a dark town suit.

'You must have a cup of coffee before you start dancing,' said Mrs Barlow, leading them to the buffet table.

Mr Jones took his cup of coffee and suddenly recognised the Outlaws, who were still busy on the massed array of dainties.

'My gallant rescuers!' he said. 'I'm really most grateful to you.' They grinned sheepishly through mouthfuls of chocolate cake. 'You know, when I was a boy, I had great fun getting up winter sports. I think I'll try one of those delicious sandwiches. The Mad Hatter ought to have a sandwich, oughtn't he, and this careless son of mine left it in the car . . . Well, now, you boys ought to try winter sports. My son has some skis and a good toboggan put away somewhere. We'll dig them out. And I know a grand place for you to have winter sports – that field just behind my son's house. Come along tomorrow morning, all of you, and we'll have the time of our lives. I know that my son had to forbid some wretched little hooligans from using the field, but this is quite a different matter, isn't it, Aloysius?'

Aloysius blinked at the Outlaws for some moments in silence, then:

'Er – yes,' he said. 'Yes, yes, yes, yes, yes.'

Chapter 2

William and the Nature Ramble

'Of course you must go, William,' said Mrs Brown.

'Why should I?' said William. 'I've got more important things to do than go nature ramblin'.'

'What have you got to do?'

'Well, I can't think of anythin' at the minute,' admitted William, 'but I know I have. Gosh!' – with a snort of contempt – 'Nature ramblin'! It's jus' a waste of valu'ble time.'

'Nonsense, William!' said Mrs Brown. 'It's – it's educational.'

'Well, I get enough of that in school' said William bitterly, 'without them startin' on me outside.'

'But you ought to *want* to learn about wild flowers, dear.'

'Well, I don't,' said William firmly. 'I'm not int'rested in 'em. I'm int'rested in *live* nature like frogs an' rats an' insects an' tadpoles an' caterpillars, but I'm not int'rested in flowers. Gosh!' (repeating his snort of contempt). 'Flowers! They don't do anythin'. Tadpoles turn into frogs an' caterpillars turn into butterflies an' rats an' frogs do jolly int'restin' things, but flowers jus' don't do anythin' at all. If they started turnin' into somethin' else or jumpin' about or learnin' tricks, I might be int'rested in 'em, but they don't, so I'm not.'

'It's no good arguing, William. You're expected to go and you must go. It's very kind of Dr Ellison to give the prize.'

The late General Ellison, who had been a governor of the school that William attended, had been an ardent botanist and had given a prize of ten shillings each year to the best collection of local flora made by any boy of eleven or under – the search to be carried out on a single afternoon during the summer term. Neither staff nor pupils were enthusiastic and it had been hoped, on the general's death, that the whole thing might be dropped, but his son offered to continue to present the prize in his father's memory, and no one liked to refuse the offer.

General Ellison's son was a doctor with a large practice in Marleigh and, though he had shared his father's interest in local flora, he had little time nowadays to devote to it. So the affair dragged on from year to year, the only flicker of interest being roused by the thought of the ten-shilling prize, which was always presented to the winner on the spot.

'I suppose you must have something to put them in,' went on Mrs Brown. 'The plants, I mean.'

'Dunno,' said William indifferently. 'Crispie's takin' us an' he didn't say so. He doesn't know anythin' about nature, anyway. Ole Stinks gen'rally takes us, but he's got 'flu an' they've put it on to ole Crispie 'cause they know he daren't say "no".'

Mr Crisp was a temporary master who had come down

from Oxford the previous year. He was putting in time with temporary teaching jobs till he should have established himself as one of the foremost literary figures of the day. He couldn't make up his mind whether to establish himself as a poet or novelist (in both of which capacities he considered that he already outstripped most of his contemporaries) and he was supremely uninterested in his pupils.

'I think you'd better take a case of some sort,' said Mrs Brown. 'Now go and get clean and tidy while I find something.'

After a lengthy search she discovered an old attaché case of Mr Brown's in the cupboard under the stairs and an ancient fork and trowel at the back of the tool shed. She was pathetically anxious that William should be properly equipped for his expedition. She always cherished a wistful, and as yet unfulfilled, hope that he might one day acquit himself creditably on some public occasion. Then she went upstairs to put the finishing – and much needed – touches to the process of cleaning and tidying.

'You'll do your best, won't you, William?' she said as he followed her downstairs, his face wearing an expression of deep gloom. 'Here's a case to put the specimens in and a fork and trowel to dig them up with. And it's time you started now.'

She handed him the case and stood looking at him. He was clean. He was tidy. He was setting off for a nature ramble like any ordinary well-conducted child. But nonetheless faint doubts stirred at the back of her mind.

'You won't get into any mischief, will you, William?' she said.

'Me?' said William. He seemed pained and surprised by the suggestion. 'Of course not.'

'You'll just – collect plants and things?'

''Course,' said William.

'You won't – get rough or anything?'

'Me?' said William. Again he seemed pained and surprised by the suggestion. ' '*Course* not.'

'Good-bye, then, dear. Have a nice time and – er – find some nice plants.'

'G'-bye,' said William.

He set off down the road, carrying his case. Mrs Brown stood at the window and watched him. He was a neat decorous figure, his hair sleekly brushed, his stockings firmly gartered. But the faint doubts still stirred at the back of her mind.

William collected Ginger, Henry and Douglas, and the four set off to the appointed meeting-place in Marleigh woods. Mr Crisp was already there. He carried a brief-case that contained the first two chapters of the novel that was to burst like a thunder-clap on the astonished world. He'd got stuck in the middle of the second chapter and couldn't see his way out. Moreover, he wasn't quite satisfied with what he had already written. He had read somewhere that the chief mark of distinction in a modern writer was the use of unusual metaphors and he couldn't think of any. He'd borrowed several from Proust but he felt that he ought to have a few of his own. He wanted to compare the heroine's smile to something but he couldn't think what. He hoped that a quiet afternoon in the leafy seclusion of the wood might give him inspiration.

The boys were making their way towards him along the paths – James Pinchin, Frankie Parsons, Victor

Jameson, Frankie Dakers, Jimmy Barlow and the rest. They looked earnest and a little bored. Mr Crisp gave them the supercilious stare that hid his secret fear of them.

'What shall we do, sir?' said Frankie Parsons.

'Ramble,' said Mr Crisp curtly. 'That's what you're here for, isn't it?' He assumed his newly acquired school-master manner. 'Collect any – er – flora that take your fancy in the course of your rambling and bring them to me when you hear the whistle. Meanwhile leave me in peace.'

'Can't we come and ask you what things are, sir?' said Victor Jameson.

'No,' said Mr Crisp.

'Why not?' said Frankie.

'Because I shouldn't know,' said Mr Crisp in a tone of quiet triumph.

He sat down with his back against an oak tree and opened his brief-case. The nature ramblers straggled off down the woodland paths.

Ginger, Henry and Douglas gathered round William. There was a suggestion of suppressed excitement about William. His air of gloom had vanished.

'What'll we do, William?' said Ginger.

'I've got a jolly good idea,' said William. 'It's come to me quite sudden. We'll go over the road to the woods on the other side an' play Red Indians.'

'I dunno that we ought to,' said Henry.

'We're s'posed to be doin' nature,' said Douglas.

'Well, Red Indians *are* nature,' said William. 'Gosh! They're nat'ral, aren't they? Come to that, they're more nat'ral than flowers. It's a jolly sight more nat'ral to fight than jus' to sit about doin' nothin' same as flowers. Come on!'

Discarding their few lingering scruples, the Outlaws set off to the end of the wood and crossed the road to the farther wood.

'Now we'll find a place for the Red Indian camp an' a place for the ranch,' said William, 'an' Henry an' Douglas can be cowboys first an' Ginger an' me Red Indians, then we'll change round.' He opened his case and took out the fork and fern trowel. 'These'll do for tomahawks. It was a jolly good idea of my mother's to put 'em in . . . I'll be Chief Hawk Eye.'

'All right, an' I'll be Chief Eagle Nose,' said Ginger.

'No, you can't be. You can't have two chiefs in the same tribe.'

'Yes, you can.'

'No, you can't.'

'You can.'

'You can't. You can be Assistant Chief Eagle Nose, if you like.'

Ginger considered. Argument with William was useless and physical combat generally inconclusive. And he wanted to get on with the game.

'All right,' he said, 'if you'll salute when you speak to me.'

'All right,' said William, 'if you'll salute when you speak to me.'

'All right.'

They found suitable clearings for the ranch and the Red Indian camp and at first all went well. William and Ginger crawled on all fours though the grass, made a sudden attack on Henry and Douglas, brandishing tomahawks and uttering blood-curdling war cries, scalped them and dragged them back to their camp. After that William and Ginger exchanged military salutes and the scene was laid for the next attack, in which, after a lengthy and spirited fight, Henry and Douglas captured and scalped William and Ginger. But when next William and Ginger crawled through the grass and rose to the attack, the ranchers put up no defence. Instead, Henry looked round uneasily and said, 'I say, William, there's girls about.'

'*Girls?*' said William, his face stiffening in horror.

'Yes, we've seen 'em through the trees. They've got green skirts an' white blouses on. They're those awful girls from Rose Mount School.'

'We'll jolly well keep out of their way, then,' said William. 'Where are they?'

'They seem to've gone now,' said Henry. 'We jus' saw them goin' along the path. They didn't see us. I s'pect it's all right.'

'Come on, then,' said William. 'You attack one side of the ranch, Assistant Chief Eagle Nose, an' I'll attack the other. Come on! *At* 'em!'

Raising their war cry, brandishing their tomahawks, the two fell upon the ranchers and dragged them down the path to the camp.

And then they stood, transfixed by amazement. For a little girl was sitting there as if awaiting their arrival. She had bright red hair, a snub nose and a determined expression.

'Get out!' said William fiercely. 'You've no right here.'

'Yes, I have,' said the little girl. 'Miss Pink's taking us on a nature ramble in the wood, and she said we could go anywhere we liked, so I came here.'

'Well, you can jolly well get out of here,' said William. 'We're Red Indians.'

'Yes, I know you are,' said the little girl. 'I've been watching you. I'm your squaw.'

For a moment the power of speech deserted William, then he advanced on her, his features twisted into a startling expression of ferocity, his tomahawk held threateningly aloft.

'Get *out*!' he said between his teeth. 'Get out or we'll scalp you an' – an' skin you an' – an' roast you an' – an' eat you an'—'

'That's cannibals,' said the little girl placidly. 'You've got mixed. Red Indians don't eat people.'

William's expression of ferocity had relaxed, not because he felt any less outraged but because the muscles of his face refused any longer to endure the strain it imposed on them.

He glared at her.

'Get out,' he repeated a little lamely. 'Get out or – or – or—'

'Don't be silly,' said the girl in a tone of sweet reasonableness. 'If you're Red Indians you've got to have a squaw to cook your food for you and I'm going to be your squaw and cook your food for you. My name's Isabella, so I'm Squaw Isabella. Now go off and have another fight and when you come back I'll have cooked your food for you.'

William tried to resume his expression of ferocity but all he cold manage was a squint and bared clenched teeth.

'If you've not gone when we come back,' he said, 'we'll – we'll—'

'Good-bye,' said the girl. 'Don't be late for dinner.'

Not knowing quite what else to do, they set off again down the path to the ranch.

'I bet we scared her,' said William with a short laugh. 'I bet we scared her all right.'

'Yes, I bet we curdled all the blood in her veins with terror,' said Henry.

'I bet she's running away now as fast as she can,' said Ginger, imitating William's short laugh.

'Yes, I bet we never see *her* again,' said Douglas.

But they spoke without conviction. The fight was a half-hearted one, the war cries feeble, attacked and attackers spiritless and preoccupied. They made their way slowly, very slowly, back along the path towards the clearing.

'I bet she'll have gone, all right,' said William.

'Yes, we needn't worry about *her* any more,' said Ginger.

None of them was surprised, however, to find the self-appointed squaw bustling about the clearing in a proprietary fashion when they reached it. What did surprise them was the sight of four picnic plates containing lettuce and sandwiches.

'Gosh!' said William faintly.

'Come along,' said their squaw imperiously. 'I've cooked your food. Eat it up. And don't make crumbs. I want to keep the place tidy.'

Helplessly they sat down and began to eat the lettuce and sandwiches, while the squaw continued to bustle about the clearing, picking up twigs and dead leaves and throwing them into the bushes. The sandwiches were delicious – sardine, tomato, cheese and egg. The Outlaws ate them in bewildered silence.

'Well – er – thanks,' said William at last, rising to his feet. 'And now—'

'COME ALONG,' SAID THEIR SQUAW IMPERIOUSLY. 'EAT IT UP. AND
DON'T MAKE CRUMBS.'

'Go and have another fight,' ordered the squaw. 'I'll
have some more food cooked for you when you come
back.'

Dazedly they set off and had another fight. It was even
more half-hearted than the last.

'We'll never shake her off now,' said William gloomily.

'She might jus' get bored an' go away,' said Ginger. 'My mother says she gets bored to screaming sobs with housework.'

'*She* won't,' said Henry. 'She's one of those super-women like Boadicea an' Mrs Beeton.'

'They were jolly good sandwiches,' said Douglas.

Again they made their way along the path to the clearing. The squaw had found a small fallen branch from a fir tree and was vigorously sweeping out the clearing with it. On the picnic plates stood little piles of cakes.

'Wipe your feet,' she ordered shrilly. 'I don't want muddy footmarks all over the place. That piece of long grass there is the doormat.'

William hesitated, then suddenly his manhood asserted itself.

'No, we jolly well won't wipe our feet,' he said.

'Then you haven't any manners,' said the squaw severely. 'Everyone with manners wipes their feet. Oh, well' – she shrugged – 'I can't help it if you haven't any manners. Here's your food. Eat it quickly and get back to your fight.'

William was seized by an almost overpowering impulse to fling the little girl from the clearing, and the cakes after her, but the cakes were iced cakes with cherries on the top and the impulse died away.

They ate the cakes in silence and made their way back to the other clearing.

'I almost wish we'd stuck to plants,' said Ginger.

'Yes, she's a jolly sight worse than nature,' agreed William.

'We could jus' go off an' find another place,' suggested Henry.

But somehow they were reluctant to leave the adventure in this unfinished state.

'We might as well see what she's got for us next,' said Ginger.

'Those cakes were jolly good,' said Douglas.

In a sort of dream they went from ranch to camp, from camp to ranch. They found chocolate biscuits, gingerbreads, cheese straws.

'Gosh!' said William helplessly. 'It jus' seems to go on an' on an' on. It can't go on for *ever*.'

And it didn't.

On their next visit to the camp they found the plates empty and the little girl in tears.

'What's the matter?' said William.

She turned a flushed angry face to them.

'You nasty, horrid, *greedy* boys!' she said. 'You've eaten *everything*.'

They stared at her open-mouthed.

'Well, you gave it to us,' said William. 'Gosh! You *gave* it us.'

'There's nothing left. Miss Pink will be furious. You *beastly* boys to eat it all up!'

'Well, what was it?' said Ginger.

'It was the picnic tea for the nature ramble. Matron packed it and Miss Pink told me to stay by the basket – it's over there behind that bush – and guard it and you've gone and eaten it all up and they'll be *furious*.'

'B-but you *gave* it us,' said William again.

'Well, I thought I'd just take a little bit that they wouldn't notice it had gone and I kept on just taking a little bit and I thought they wouldn't notice it had gone and now it's *all* gone. I've suddenly found I've got to the bottom and there's nothing left and you've eaten it all up, you horrid, beastly, *greedy* boys!'

'We couldn't help it,' said William.

'Yes, you could,' stormed the little girl tearfully. 'Of *course* you could. People can help *eating*, can't they? Don't be stupid. You're horrid, beastly, *greedy* boys. And you've got to get me some more. *You've* eaten it and you've got to get me some more.'

'All right, we will,' said William with dignity. 'Makin' all this fuss about a bit of food! 'Course we'll get you some more. Why did you give it us, anyway?'

'I wanted to be a squaw and cook ven'son for Red Indians,' said the little girl, 'and—'

'It wasn't ven'son, anyway,' put in Henry.

'Well, I was *pretending* it was and now I'm going to get into an awful row and it's all your fault.'

She burst into another stormy fit of sobbing.

'Oh, shut up!' said William desperately. 'We're goin' to get you some food, aren't we?' He snatched up his attaché case from a corner of the clearing and turned to the gaping Outlaws. 'Come on. Let's go an' get her some more food.'

They followed him down the path to the end of the wood. There they stopped to consider the situation.

'We *can't* get her any more food, William,' said Ginger. 'We haven't any money.'

'I've got half a crown,' said Henry. 'My aunt gave it me this mornin' but I'm jolly well not goin' to spend it on *her*.'

'I should think not!' said William. 'Gosh! I never want to see another girl for the rest of my life.'

'Well, you promised to get some food for her,' said Ginger, 'an' I don't know how you're goin' to do it.'

'Oh, it's easy enough,' said William airily. 'What did she start with?'

'Salad,' said Henry.

'Well, salad's easy enough,' said William. It's jus' green stuff. There's plenty of green stuff about.' He looked around him. 'Here's some sorrel. Sorrel's salad. I've know grown-up people put sorrel in salad, so it mus' be all right.' He opened his attaché case. 'Shove it in . . . And here's some dandelion leaves. I've known grown-up people put those in, too, so they mus' be all right. Shove 'em in. And here's some nettles. People eat nettles.'

'They don't,' said Ginger.

'Yes, they do. My mother met someone once that'd made soup of them an' she said it was delicious. Hold 'em tight so they won't sting you. Shove 'em in . . . An' there's some dock leaves. They go with nettles. Shove 'em in.' A spirit of recklessness seized him. 'Come on. I bet all this green stuff's salad. It's what nature meant people to eat or it wouldn't have grown it. Shove it in.'

The spirit of recklessness infected the others.

'Shove this in,' said Henry taking up a handful of groundsel. 'Canaries eat it, so it mus' be food.'

'Here's a pink flower that looks jolly good,' said Douglas.

'Shove it in,' said William. 'Shove 'em all in.' He tore up a handful of grass and weeds, rammed them into the case and inspected the final result. 'I think that's enough salad. We've got to leave room for some solid food. She gave us some solid food, so we've got to give her some.'

'An' how're we goin' to *get* any solid food?' said Ginger sarcastically. 'Kin'ly tell me that.'

'I'm jolly well not goin' to spend my half-crown on it,' said Henry.

'All right, we're not askin' you to,' said William. 'Gosh! Anyone can find a bit of solid food.'

'How?' challenged Ginger.

'Give me time to *think*,' said William irritably. 'My brain's only *yuman* same as everyone else's . . . Come on. Let's go along the Marleigh road an' I bet I get an idea, all right. I'm jolly good at gettin' ideas. I can almost feel one comin' now.'

They climbed over the stile at the end of the wood and walked along the Marleigh road. William walked with set stern countenance, his lips compressed, his eyes glaring, his brows drawn closely together.

'Has it come yet, William?' said Ginger.

'Oh, shut up!' said William. 'I keep tellin' you I've got to have time to *think*. I bet that man that invented rockets didn't have people botherin' him all the time he was thinkin', askin' if it'd come yet. I bet—'

He stopped suddenly and peered through a hole in the hedge that surrounded a small neat garden. Then he turned to the others. His brow had cleared.

'I've *got* it!' he said triumphantly. 'Look!'

They joined him, crowding round the hole, scuffling for the best position.

'A lot of flowers . . .' said Ginger in a puzzled voice.

'A silly stone rabbit . . .' said Douglas.

'A bit of washin' on the line . . .' said Henry.

'But *look*, you chumps!' said William, his excitement rising. 'A bird-table! People sometimes put jolly good food on bird-tables. I once knew a woman that put a whole *cake* on one. I'll go in an' have a look. You stay here. It might make someone suspicious if we all went in.'

It might have made anyone suspicious had they seen William insinuate himself through the hole in the hedge, crawl, Red-Indian fashion, over the short grass of the lawn, take cover for a moment behind the stone rabbit, spring to his feet, transfer the contents of the bird-table to his pocket, then return on all fours to his hole. But it happened that the occupant of the house had gone to London for a day's shopping and there were no witnesses of the scene except Ginger, Henry and Douglas.

'It's not much,' he said as he rejoined them, 'but it's not bad. Some pieces of bread an' a nice bit of bun with two currants in it. It's solid food, anyway.'

'It's wrong to steal from birds,' said Douglas piously, as William opened the case and put his pieces into it.

'Gosh!' said William indignantly. 'I like that. I jolly well *like* that! Birds!' He returned to an ancient grievance. 'They get *everythin'* done for them. Food put out for them all over the place. People watchin' them an' – an' makin' picture postcards of 'em an' – an' imitatin' their noises on the wireless . . . an' all they do is fly about an' build nests. Gosh! No one does anythin' like that for *boys* an' it's time they started. It's time they started havin' *boy*-tables in their gardens an'—'

'Well, never mind that now,' said Ginger, knowing that William, mounted on one of his hobby-horses, could go on for ever. 'We've got other things to think of now.'

'A'right,' said William, ramming home the catches of his case, 'but it isn't fair, all the same. They ought to eat off nature same as they were meant to. Bird-tables aren't *nat'ral*. Now boy-tables *are* nat'ral. 'Least, they ought to be nat'ral. 'Least—'

'Come on,' said Douglas, throwing an apprehensive glance into the garden. 'Come on before anyone comes out.'

They walked down the road till they reached two cottages – one white-washed, the other pink-washed. As they approached, a car drew up and a long thin man with a long thin harassed-looking face got out. Without glancing at the boys, he entered the pink-washed cottage.

'Gosh!' said William. 'Dr Ellison! It's a good thing he didn't see us. We're s'posed to be nature ramblin' after his prize.'

'We'd better go off quick,' said Douglas.

'No, it's all right, said William. 'He's gone to see ole Mrs Richards an' she tells him all her troubles an' he can't get away. When my mother had 'flu he told her that he couldn't ever get away from Mrs Richards 'cause she told him all her troubles, so we needn't hurry.'

'There's a bird-table here,' said Henry, craning his neck to look over the hedge into the garden of the whitewashed cottage, 'but I can see the top of it an' it's empty. The birds must have eaten everything that was on it.'

'They would,' said William bitterly. 'They—'

'Shut up!' said Ginger. 'Put your heads down an' shut up.'

They lowered their heads and peered through the hedge. The door of the cottage had opened and a small grey-haired woman had emerged, carrying a bowl heaped with pieces of sandwiches, pastry and cake. Miss Hampshire had had some friends in to coffee that morning and had over-estimated their appetites. She poured the scraps on to the bird-table and returned to the house, closing the door behind her.

'Come on!' said William. 'Let's get it quick. I'll go. I'll take the case an' shove the stuff in.'

'She'll see you,' said Ginger.

'No, she won't,' said William. 'I'll do it so quick she won't have time.'

The hedge was thick-grown at the top but sparse about the roots. William squeezed himself through, dragged the case after him, made his way boldly to the bird-table, swept the contents into the case and returned.

'I've done it. She didn't see.'

'Come on away quick,' said Douglas.

But a sort of fascination held them to the spot. The back door was opening again and Miss Hampshire was coming out with a plate that contained the remainder of the coffee-party left-overs. Her face wore a dreamy little smile (she had enjoyed the coffee-party) as she approached the bird-table. Then the smile froze and her mouth dropped open. She stared incredulously at the empty floor of the bird-table. She drew her hand over it to make sure that her eyes were not deceiving her. She looked up at the sky. She looked round at the trees. There were no birds in sight. Then she saw the four heads that the Outlaws had raised incautiously over the top of the hedge and began slowly to approach them.

'Slip the case into Dr Ellison's car, Ginger,' whispered William, thrusting the case at him. 'It's all right. Mrs Richards won't have finished her troubles yet.'

Ginger put the case into the car and joined the others. Miss Hampshire was gazing at them in helpless bewilderment.

'Er – have you seen any of my little feathered friends?' she said.

'HAVE YOU SEEN ANY OF MY LITTLE FEATHERED FRIENDS?'
ASKED MISS HAMPSHIRE.

'No,' said William.

'You haven't seen a *flock* of my little feathered friends descend suddenly on the bird-table and then fly off?'

'No,' said Ginger.

'You haven't noticed any *rats* about, have you?'

'No,' said Henry.

'It couldn't be rats, because there aren't any rats about. You – you haven't seen any large and unusual bird such as – well, such as a Great Crested Grebe descend on the bird-table and make a clean sweep of it? I expect they have enormous appetites, and eat at an enormous speed.'

'No,' said Douglas.

'I must really write to *The Feathered World* about it. You – you've none of you noticed anything *strange* going on, have you?'

'No,' said the Outlaws.

The blank imbecility of their expressions would have roused suspicion in anyone who knew them, but, fortunately for them, Miss Hampshire did not know them. It was obvious, however, that her bewilderment was transferring itself from the bird-table to the boys.

'What are you doing here?' she said.

'We're goin' to the woods,' said William, intensifying the imbecility of his expression and adding a glassy smile as he began to sidle away. 'G'-bye.'

They went off down the road. After a few yards William looked back. Miss Hampshire had opened her garden gate and stood there, gazing after them thoughtfully.

'Good thing we put the case in the car!' said William. 'I bet she'd have made us open it.'

They walked on a few more yards then turned round again. Miss Hampshire had gone back into her cottage. The gate was closed. The garden was empty. The doctor's car still stood outside.

'Nip back an' get the case, Ginger,' said William. 'I'd better not go 'cause I've got a sort of feelin' she was beginnin' to think I'd got somethin' to do with it.'

They walked on towards the entrance to the wood. In a few moments Ginger rejoined them with the case. Urged by a sudden impulse of flight, they ran to the stile and scrambled over it.

'That's gone off jolly well,' said William. He began to

swagger down the path. 'I *told* you I'd get an idea an' I did an' it was a jolly good one. Now all we have to do is to find that girl an' give it her. We'd better tidy it first. I bet the salad an' solid food's got a bit mixed up. Let's go behind this bush an' sort it out.'

They went behind the bush. William put the case on the ground. They sat round it in a circle. William opened it. It contained a stethoscope, a thermometer, a hypodermic syringe, a couple of bandages, a copy of *The Lancet* and a bottle of white pills.

'You *chump*, Ginger!' said William. 'You've brought the wrong case. You'll jolly well have to go back an' change it.'

'DR ELLISON'S CASE HAS BEEN STOLEN FROM HIS CAR. THERE ARE
DANGEROUS DRUGS IN IT,' SAID ONE OF THE WOMEN.

Douglas had taken up the bottle of pills.

'Wonder what they are,' he said. He opened it and put one of the pills in his mouth, chewing it with a critical frown.

'What's it taste like?' said Henry.

'It's got a queer sort of taste,' said Douglas.

'Sh!' said Ginger.

Footsteps sounded along the path. Two women, coming from opposite directions, met just by the bush. The Outlaws crouched down in their hiding place. The women stopped and greeted each other.

'I've just seen Dr Ellison,' said one. 'He's in an awful state. His case has been stolen from his car.'

'Tut-tut!' said the other. 'It's all this increase of crime that's at the bottom of it.'

'Yes,' said the first. 'He said that the thief had left a case of garbage in its place.'

'Garbage!' muttered William indignantly.

'He's going to the police about it. He's terribly worried because he said there were some dangerous drugs in it.'

'Well, well,' said the other. 'You never know what people will do next, do you?'

They went their separate ways. William, Henry and Ginger turned to look at Douglas. A greenish hue had overspread his face.

'D-dangerous d-drugs . . .' he stammered.

They stared at him in mounting consternation.

'What d'you feel like?' said William.

'I don't know,' said Douglas. His eyes were wide with horror. 'I think I feel a bit funny.'

'You mus' be poisoned,' said William. He rose to his feet. 'Come on. We've got to do somethin' about it.'

'Shall we take him to the doctor?' said Henry.

'No, we can't waste time takin' him to the doctor's,' said William. 'We've got to do somethin' quick. It's a matter of life an' death.'

'What can we do?' said Ginger.

'Make him sick,' said William. 'That's what you do with poisoned people. You make 'em sick. He was sick with ice-creams once. We might try that again. We'll go to Bentley's. Come on. We'll have to spend that half-crown of yours now Henry.'

'All right,' said Henry a little glumly.

They set off again to Marleigh. William walked on one side of Douglas, Ginger and Henry on the other. They kept their eyes fixed on him anxiously as they walked. Douglas stared in front of him, an expression of blank misery on his face.

'Are you feelin' any funnier?' said William.

'Yes, I think I am a bit,' said Douglas.

'You take his arm, Ginger,' said William, 'an' I'll take the other. We mustn't let him use up all his strength. I don't s'pose he's got much left. D'you feel you're gettin' weaker, Douglas?'

'Yes, I think I do a bit,' said Douglas, the look of misery on his face deepening to panic.

William clutched one arm, Ginger the other, and Douglas allowed himself to be dragged along between them in a posture of extreme discomfort.

'You cert'nly do seem to be gettin' weaker,' said William. 'You can hardly walk at all now, can you?'

'No,' agreed Douglas.

'Gosh!' said William. 'We'll have to be quick.'

Mr Bentley's shop, besides a large assortment of sweets, contained several dishes of unhealthy-looking cakes, a glass jug of bright red liquid and an ice-cream refrigerator. In one corner of the shop was an ancient metal table surrounded by four ancient metal chairs.

William and Ginger dumped their burden on one of them and William went up to the counter.

'A fourpenny ice-cream, please,' he said.

He took the ice-cream to the table and set it in front of Douglas.

'Eat it quick,' he said, 'before the poison gets hold of you.'

'An' does its deadly work,' said Henry.

Mr Bentley, standing behind his counter, was mildly surprised by the sight of three boys watching with tense, set faces a fourth boy eating an ice-cream.

'Do you feel sick?' said William as Douglas swallowed the last mouthful.

'DO YOU FEEL SICK?' ASKED WILLIAM.

'No,' said Douglas after a moment's consideration. 'I still feel funny, but I don't feel sick.'

'We'll have to give him another,' said William.

Again their gaze followed every movement of the unhappy Douglas as he ate his way through the ice-cream.

'Well, d'you feel sick now?' said William.

'Not axshully *sick*,' said Douglas.

'Gosh, he'll have to have another,' said William.

The process was repeated for a third time, then for a fourth.

'D'you feel sick *now*?' said William with a faint note of exasperation in his voice.

'No,' said Douglas.

'That's one an' fourpence gone,' said Henry gloomily.

'Yes, it's not much good goin' on with ice-creams,' said William. 'Let's try him on the cakes.'

He approached the counter and examined the plates of dainties with a critical frown.

'How much are these?' he said, pointing to a pile of confectionery that seemed to consist of blobs of marsh-mallow on a sugar basis, with strings of coconut sticking out at random, and that bore the label, 'Coconut Wizards'.

'Threepence each,' said Mr Bentley. 'How many do you want?'

'One,' said William, taking one and laying threepence on the counter.

'You can have a plate,' said Mr Bentley.

'We're not payin' anythin' extra for plates,' said William. 'It's comin' expensive enough without that.'

'Plates are free,' said Mr Bentley, 'unless you eat 'em.'

William plumped the plate in front of Douglas.

'Go on. Eat it,' he said.

'I'm feelin' a bit funnier,' said Douglas after the sec-ond cake, 'but I'm not feelin' axshully *sick* yet.'

It was evident that the patience of the three was wear-ing a little thin.

'Gosh!' said William. 'Here we are spendin' all this money on you an' you aren't even *tryin'* to feel sick.'

'I am, William,' said the wretched Douglas. 'I'm tryin' as hard as I can.'

'Well, eat another an' see what you feel like then,' said William.

'Eat it slowly,' said Ginger.

'No eat it quick,' said William.

Douglas finished the last crumb and sat staring into the distance, a glazed look in his eyes.

'I'm not quite sure,' he said, 'but I *think* I'm beginnin' to feel sick. Jus' beginnin'.'

Their spirits rose.

'Let's give him another an' make sure of it,' said William.

'Not much left of the half-crown,' said Henry.

'There's twopence,' said Ginger.

'What do you feel like now?' they said expectantly as Douglas put the last string of coconut into his mouth.

'Not much diff'rent,' said Douglas.

'Tell you what!' said William. 'Let's give him a drink of raspberry fizz to wash it down an' mix it up.' He went to the counter again. 'Twopenny drink of raspberry fizz, please.'

Mr Bentley poured some of the bright red liquid into a cardboard carton.

They watched Douglas intently as he drank it.

'Well?' said William.

'Yes, I think I am feelin' a bit sicker,' said Douglas. 'I think it's comin'.'

'Good!' said William. 'One more Coconut Wizard ought to finish him.' Once more he approached the counter. 'Another Coconut Wizard, please.'

'Where's your money?' said Mr Bentley.

'We haven't any,' said William. 'We'll pay you on Sat'day.'

'No,' said Mr Bentley.

William fixed him a stern gaze.

'It's a matter of life and death,' he said. 'That boy's been poisoned.

'I'll say he has!' said Mr Bentley.

'By dangerous drugs,' said Ginger.

'Look here! I've had about enough of you lot,' said Mr Bentley. 'Clear out.'

'You'll have his death on your hands,' said Henry in a tone of solemn warning. 'It'll lie at your door an'—'

'Clear *out*!' said Mr Bentley, opening the flap of his counter.

'Come on!' said William.

They made a hasty exit from the shop.

'Serve him jolly well right if Douglas *did* die of it!' said William indignantly.

Douglas gave a faint moan of protest. He was blinking distractedly.

'He looks a bit worse,' said Ginger hopefully.

'I think we ought to take him to Dr Ellison,' said Henry. 'We don't want to leave it till he's past help. Dangerous drugs work their way up from the stomach to the brain an' I bet they're jolly near Douglas's brain now. He looks as if they were anyway!'

Douglas gave another faint moan.

'Well, he's out on his rounds now,' said William, looking up and down the road. 'He's left Mrs Richards' an' we dunno where he is.'

But at that moment the doctor's car came along the road, slowing down by the petrol pump that was next to Mr Bentley's shop. He looked carelessly at the boys then fastened his eyes on the case that Ginger was still carrying.

'Good Lord!' he said, stopping the car and leaping out of it. 'That's my case.'

'Yes, I'm sorry,' said William. 'We took it by mistake for ours.'

'What on earth do you mean!' said Dr Ellison angrily.

He snatched the case from Ginger, opened it and began to check the contents.

'The d-dangerous d-drugs . . .' stammered Douglas.

'There aren't any,' snapped the doctor. 'I thought there were at first but I went back to the surgery to make sure and I found that I hadn't put them in.'

'Th-th-th-those . . .' stammered Douglas, pointing to the bottle of pills.

'A harmless indigestion preparation,' said the doctor.

'Gosh!' said William.

They turned accusing eyes on Douglas.

'A whole half-crown!' said Henry. 'Jus' *wasted*!'

'Well, I couldn't help it,' said Douglas. 'I *did* feel funny. I still do.'

'May we have our case, please?' said William, taking it from the car and adding coldly, 'an' it's not garbage.'

The doctor's emotion had been gathering force. His voice rose to a bellow.

'What do you mean by it, you young—'

A whistle cut sharply through the air.

The doctor started.

'What on earth's that?' he said.

'It's Mr Crisp,' said William. 'He said he'd blow a whistle at five o'clock for the end of the nature ramble.'

'Nature ramble?' said the doctor.

'Yes, we've been nature ramblin' for the Ellison prize,' said William.

The doctor stared at him.

'Good Heavens!' he said. 'I ought to be there. They rang me up last night and I said I'd be there at five o'clock to judge the specimens. It went clean out of my mind. Good *Heavens*!'

He flung the case into the car, locked the doors and set off towards the stile that led into the wood. The sound of the whistle seemd to have driven the little affair of the case, too, clean out of his mind. He made no reference to it as he climbed the stile and strode along the path.

The Outlaws followed, their progress slightly delayed by Douglas, who left them abruptly to dive behind a bush. When he rejoined them, his face, though pallid, wore an expression of smug self-satisfaction.

'I've been sick, William,' he said proudly.

'Oh, shut up!' said William. 'We're jus' about sick of you bein' sick an' not bein' sick an'—'

'Gosh, look!' whispered Ginger.

A bend in the path had brought them to a group of Rose Mount girls clustered round Miss Pink. Miss Pink was large and floppy and vague-looking.

'I've just had a message from Lady Markham,' she was saying. 'Evidently she rang up the school this morning and asked us all to go to tea to the Manor after the nature ramble. The message never reached Matron or me, but, of course, we'll go there now we know about it. I've forgotten where we left the basket of provisions that Matron made up.' She turned a large vague smile on to Isabella. 'You were in charge of it, dear, weren't you? I don't know what we'd better do with the food.' The large vague smile floated towards the Outlaws. 'Perhaps these little boys would like it?'

'They did,' said Isabella. She shot a baleful glance at the four boys. 'They said it wasn't ven'son and they wouldn't wipe their feet, and—'

'Come on quick,' said William. 'She's startin' again.'

They hurried down the path after the doctor till they

came to the clearing where Mr Crisp stood, surrounded
by the returned ramblers.

'So sorry to have kept you waiting,' said the doctor in a
brisk business-like voice. 'I'm a busy man you know, and
a doctor can't cut short his patients' consultations. I've
come along as soon as I could manage it. Now let's see
what you've all got.'

He opened tins, boxes, plastic bags and gave short terse
reports on the contents.

'Pimpernel, tormentil . . . nothing of much interest
here . . . hogwort . . . notice the large umbel and different
sizes of blossom . . . hare's trefoil . . . notice the two
pointed stipules . . . woodvetch . . . dyer's greenwood
. . . notice the lanceolated leaf . . . used for dyeing in the
old days . . . leopard's bane . . . hedge calamint . . . notice
the thirteen longitudinal ridges of the calyx . . . stachys
. . . bladder campion . . . nothing out of the ordinary so far
. . . harebell . . . fleabane . . . all quite ordinary plants . . .
Have I had everyone's?' He looked round and saw
Ginger, still holding the case. 'Oh, no, there's one more.'
He took the case and opened it. 'A pity you've got the
remains of your picnic tea mixed up with the specimens.'
He brushed the contents of Miss Hampshire's bird-table
on to the ground. 'Now let's look at the specimens . . .
sorrel . . . nettles . . . clover . . . all very ordinary specimens, of course . . . There are fifteen to twenty varieties
of clover . . . one of its old names is meadow honeysuckle
because the flower heads are so rich in honey that
children will pick them to suck the honey from them,
though that, of course, is neither here nor there . . . dock
. . . dandelion . . . groundsel, of no interest at all . . .'
Then he took out a drooping pink flower and his eyes

widened. 'Good Heavens! A pink brooklime ... a pink brooklime ... *Most* interesting ... There are sixteen different species of brooklime, but the pink one is extremely rare. I've never been able to discover one myself. Who found it?'

'He did,' said William, pushing Douglas forward.

'I congratulate you, my boy,' said the doctor. 'It will be a most valuable addition to your collection. I hope that you will use the utmost care in pressing it. I must say I envy you your discovery.'

'You can have it if you like,' said William. 'He doesn't want it.'

'Don't you really, my boy?' said the doctor to Douglas.

Douglas shook his head dazedly.

'That's very good of you,' said the doctor. 'It will certainly be the gem of my collection. And, of course, there's no doubt whatever about the prize. It goes to the finder of the pink brooklime.

He handed Douglas a ten-shilling note, then turned to deliver a short speech to the boys. In it he dwelt on the enduring interest, the ever-increasing delight, to be derived from a study of the flora that are to be found in the thickets and meadows of our native land. He ended by saying how pleased he was to note the keen interest of all the boys – especially the finder of the pink brooklime – and how much he looked forward to meeting them again on the same occasion next summer.

Mr Crisp was not listening. He had sat down under his oak tree again, opened his brief-case and taken out his manuscript and pen.

'Her smile was as sweet as the meadow honeysuckle, as rare as the pink brooklime,' he wrote.

He closed his brief-case with an expression of triumphant achievement and rose to see the doctor striding off through the trees.

'Well, boys,' he said genially, 'this has been a most successful nature ramble. *Most* successful. And now it's time we all started for home.'

The boys drifted away till only William, Ginger, Henry and Douglas were left. Douglas was staring at his ten-shilling note.

'Gosh, *ten shillings*!' he said. 'What'll I do with it?'

'I'll tell you what you'll do with it,' said William grimly. 'You'll come back with us to Bentley's with it. You owe us four ice-creams, four Coconut Wizards an' a drink of raspberry fizz.'

Chapter 3

Jumble Finds a Career

'I think it's time Jumble *did* something with his life,' said William.

'Gosh! You'd think he'd done enough,' said Ginger. 'He chewed up your father's slippers yesterday.'

'Well, that wasn't his fault,' said William. 'I was tryin' to teach him to bring 'em to my father same as I saw a dog do on the pictures an' he didn't understand what I meant. He thought I meant chew 'em up. An'– Gosh! the way my father went on about 'em! You'd have thought they were made of gold or di'monds or – or that uranium stuff, the fuss he made.'

'An he ate that beef steak pie your mother made last week,' said Henry.

'Well, he thought she *meant* him to eat it,' said William. 'She put it on the draining-board an' he thought she *meant* it for him. Gosh! He wouldn't have minded givin' her a few dog biscuits. She needn't have made all that fuss 'cause he ate a bit of her ole pie.'

'An' Miss Milton said he gave her cat a nervous breakdown chasin' it,' said Douglas.

'I don't mean *that* sort of thing,' said William impatiently. 'I mean— Well, he's got the most t'rrific intelligence any dog's ever had, an' I think he ought to be trained for something.'

The Outlaws were seated on the floor of the old barn and in the centre sat Jumble, his simple face wearing a foolish and complacent expression as he listened to the discussion.

They considered the matter in silence for some moments, then Ginger said:

'We've tried to train him for things. We tried to train him for a greyhound an' he jus' walked off in the opposite direction from the one the mechanical hare was goin' in.'

'Well, he was sick of that clockwork mouse. He *knew* it wasn't a mechanical hare.'

'An' we tried to train him for a regimental mascot,' said Henry 'an' he wouldn't march with us. He jus' went in the ditch an' wouldn't come out.'

'Well he was fed up with your regimental band. That drum an' trumpet made so much noise you couldn't march to them, anyway.'

'An' we tried to train him for a St Bernard,' said Douglas.

'He was a jolly good St Bernard,' said William. 'He found me in the snow. I was covered right over with snow an' he came runnin' up an' found me.'

'Yes, 'cause you kept shoutin' to him. He couldn't help findin' you. An' anyway he'd ate up all the provisions we'd tied round his neck for you before he did find you. He ate up all the provisions when he was a husky too.'

'Well, those things were too easy for him,' said William. 'I tell you, he's got the most *t'rrific* intelligence. He's not like an ordin'ry dog.'

Jumble thumped his tail on the ground as if in agreement with the statement.

'He jus' couldn't take an int'rest in those things,'

continued William. 'We've got to find somethin' to use up his intelligence. He'd take an int'rest in it then.'

'Well, what are you going to try?' said Henry.

'We'll have to have a think,' said William, knitting his brows and assuming the expression of ferocity that accompanied his weightier mental processes.

Jumble, tiring of the discussion, yawned, scratched his ear in a comtemplative fashion and settled down to sleep.

'We'll have to think quick,' said Henry,' ''cause we've got to go to that ole party this afternoon.'

'Gosh, yes,' said Ginger. 'That ole Egerton's party.'

'Robert's goin' to do conjuring tricks at it, isn't he?' said Douglas. 'I bet he makes a mess of them.'

'You shut up, said William, rising hotly to the defence of his elder brother. 'Robert does conjuring tricks jolly well . . . 'Least,' – after a few second's consideration – 'I don't think he's ever tried before, but I bet he'll do 'em all right.' A gloomy look came over his face. 'It's all that ole Roxana . . .'

Roxana was Robert's girl friend of the moment, and Roxana's family had a young cousin, by name Egerton, staying with them while his parents were abroad. Egerton's birthday happened to fall during his visit and Roxana's family felt bound by common laws of decency to hold a party in his honour on that day. Egerton was a studious, spectacled, conscientious boy who could be trusted to cause no trouble, make no noise, wipe his feet on the mat and only speak when spoken to. But the boys of the neighbourhood, who perforce must be the guests, were of a different calibre. They were noisy and uncivilised. They fought and scuffled. They shouted. They 'got rough'.

Roxana's mother, who had a deep-rooted dislike of boys, had decided to take steps to keep the party within bounds. There should be no opportunity for fighting or scuffling or shouting or getting rough. To ensure this, she had asked an uncle of Hubert Lane's, who was supposed to be 'good with children', to open the party by a half-hour's talk, and Roxana had asked Robert to follow this by a half-hour's conjuring display, after which would come tea and a few quiet games before the guests departed in a decorous orderly fashion.

William had felt uneasy ever since he had heard of the arrangement. Hubert Lane was his inveterate foe, Hubert's uncle was breezy, hearty and, in the eyes of the Outlaws, generally destestable and, as to Robert's share in the proceedings . . . William tried not to let his mind dwell on it. Robert was a dare-devil motor cyclist, a dauntless rugger player, a persistent winner of the men's singles at the tennis club, but William doubted his ability to give a conjuring display and was afraid that the result would expose him to the jeers of his enemies and the pity of his friends.

Jumble growled softly in his sleep, recalling them to the main purpose of the meeting.

'There used to be dogs taking round milk, and turning things called spits in the old days,' said Henry vaguely.

But a light had broken out over William's sombre countenance.

'Tell you what!' he said. 'A p'lice dog.'

'Um-m,' said Ginger. 'Not a bad idea.'

'It's a wizard one,' said William. 'They've got to be jolly clever, have p'lice dogs, so it'll use up his t'rrific intelligence. Gosh! I bet he'll turn out the mos' famous p'lice dog there's ever been since the world began.'

Jumble opened one eye. It held a slight apprehensive expression, as if he suspected that plans were once more afoot for his training.

'The p'lice may not want him,' objected Ginger. 'I know he *is* intell'gent, but he's not got an intell'gent look.'

'That's his cleverness,' said William. 'He puts that on to throw people off the scent. It'll be jolly useful for a p'lice dog.'

'What are you goin' to do?' said Henry. 'Take him round to the p'lice station? I bet they won't have him. He bit that p'liceman with red hair.'

'Well, he prob'ly thought he was a crim'nal in disguise. He's got criminal's eyes, that p'liceman has, so it jus' shows how clever ole Jumble is.'

'We'd better be careful,' said Douglas. His face reflected something of the anxiety that was stealing over Jumble's. 'We don't want to get in a muddle an' end up by bein' locked up in cells an' things.'

'Oh, don't be a chump,'said William impatiently. 'We're not goin' to bother with this p'lice station here. We'll train him ourselves an' then, when we've trained him, we'll offer him to Scotland Yard. Not to live there but jus' to lend him for big cases.' William's imagination had, as usual, taken wings and was soaring to boundless heights. 'We'll start him on ordin'ry crimes – jus' little ones – an' work up gradual to rounding up international gangs an' – an' bringin' desperate murderers an' suchlike to justice.'

Jumble was now sitting bolt upright, staring at William with open mouth, his long red tongue lolling out at the corner.

'Look at him,' said William proudly. 'I bet, once he gets going, there won't be another p'lice dog in the world to touch him.'

'He's not a bloodhound build,' said Henry critically.

'Well, that makes it all the better,' said William. 'He's smaller, so he'll be able to get about quicker an' with him not lookin' like a bloodhound criminals won't be on their guard against him same as they are against bloodhounds. I think it's silly havin' bloodhounds at all 'cause crim'nals see 'em comin' an' get away in time. They'll think Jumble's jus' an ordin'ry dog. They won't know about him bein' a p'lice dog.'

'How are we goin' to start?' said Henry.

Jumble had settled down to sleep again, curling himself up into a small compass, as if hoping by this means to divert attention from himself.

William considered.

'Tell you what!' he said at last. 'Ginger an' me'll be the

'LOOK AT HIM,' SAID WILLIAM PROUDLY. 'I BET THERE WON'T BE ANOTHER P'LICE DOG IN THE WORLD TO TOUCH HIM.'

crim'nals. We'll go out an' c'mit a crime.'

'What crime?' said Douglas nervously.

'Any crime,' said William. 'It doesn't matter what crime. Any crime'll do . . . Anyway, Ginger an' me'll go an' c'mit this crime an' you an' Henry keep Jumble here an' I'll leave somethin' of mine for him to track us by. My cap'll do.' He dragged that long-suffering headgear from his pocket and handed it to Henry. 'That'll give him my scent. I bet he knows my scent already but it's best to give 'em somethin' to remind 'em. Then you wait till we've c'mitted the crime—'

'How long?' said Henry.

'Oh, not long,' said William. 'It doesn't take long to c'mit a crime. We'll only do a little one. Then you give Jumble my cap to smell an' send him off an' – an' – well, he'll track us down an' he'll have got started on his p'lice dog training.'

'Y-yes,' said Henry doubtfully, 'but s'pose you can't find a crime to commit. What'll you do then?'

'Anyone can find a crime to c'mit,' said William airily. 'There's hundreds of crimes all over the place jus' waitin' to be c'mitted. I bet sometimes real criminals don't know which to choose first.'

'Oh well,' said Douglas with a sigh of resignation, 'if we do all end up in the cells, we'll get out of that awful party this afternoon anyway.'

'Oh, shut up about that party,' said William. 'I'm tryin' to forget it. An' shut up makin' objections to everythin' I say. All you've got to do is jus' to hold Jumble till Ginger an' me have had long enough to c'mit a crime, then give him a smell of my cap an' let him go . . . Come on, Ginger.'

Jumble, waking up suddenly and realising that William

was going off without him, struggled against Douglas's and Henry's restraining hands and rent the air with indignant howls.

'He'll have to get used to it,' said William, steeling his heart against the anguish in Jumble's voice. 'He'll have to get used to goin' about a bit by himself now he's a p'lice dog.' The howls died away in the distance as the two climbed the stile and set off down the road. William looked hopefully around. 'We ought to find a crime all right. There's no one about, anyway.'

But at that moment a short plump figure rounded the bend in the road.

'Gosh! Hubert Lane!' said William.

Hubert Lane approached them with an oily smile.

'I'm looking forward to Egerton's party this afternoon, William,' he said. 'I bet Robert's goin' to be jolly funny doing conjuring tricks.'

'Oh, shut up!' said William.

'My uncle's thing's going to be jolly good,' said Hubert. 'It's stories about exciting places he's been to and exciting things he's done and it's jolly exciting . . . but I bet we'll all die of laughing at Robert's conjuring tricks.'

'Will – you – shut—' began William, but Hubert did not wait for the 'up'. He had seen the light of battle in William's eye and was running down the road as quickly as his fat legs could carry him. His mocking laugh floated back to them.

'He's not worth goin' after,' said William with a shrug. 'It wouldn't be a decent fight even if I did. He jus' starts howlin' the minute you touch him an' goes off to tell his mother.'

He turned round to watch Hubert's retreating figure.

Hubert was taking no chances. He was still running as fast as he could across the field that led to his home.

'I bet he's right, too,' said William morosely. 'I bet they will all die of laughing at Robert's tricks. 'Cept us,' he added bitterly. 'Oh well, let's get this crime done. We can't keep ole Jumble waitin' all day. There's no one about now, so—'

But two more figures were rounding the bend in the road – a young man and a girl. The young man wore a harassed, preoccupied air. The girl – a pretty girl with eyes of periwinkle blue – looked pained but patient.

'Gosh!' said William. 'Robert an' that ole Roxana!'

The couple bore down on them, so intent on their conversation that they did not notice William and Ginger till they had almost collided with them.

'Hello, Robert,' said William.

Robert threw his younger brother an angry frown.

'Can't you keep out of the way!' he snapped.

William turned and watched them gloomily.

'I bet they're talkin' about that ole conjurin' business,' he said.

William was right. They were talking about the conjuring business.

'But, Robert dear, you definitely promised to do it,' Roxana was saying. She spoke kindly but firmly and Robert felt like some hunted creature that sees the net closing round it. 'I asked you to do it and you definitely promised.'

'I know I did,' groaned Robert. 'I didn't realise . . . I didn't think . . .'

If only he had been firmer when Roxana first asked

him! He had tried to be, but she had fixed melting blue eyes on him and said 'Won't you do even this for me, Robert? I thought – I thought that you liked me just a little. Does my friendship mean nothing to you at all?'

Robert had plunged into a flowery description of what her friendship meant to him and, by the time he had finished, had found himself committed to entertaining a roomful of children by conjuring tricks at Egerton's party.

'I simply don't see the difficulty, dear,' said Roxana, still patient and reasonable. 'You've got that conjuring set I gave you, haven't you?'

'Yes,' muttered Robert.

'Have you tried it?'

'Yes, but the darn things don't work,' said Robert. 'I put things into things and they come out the same things as they went in.'

Roxana knit her delicate brows.

'I can't think why,' she said. 'Have you read the directions?'

'Of course I've read the directions,' said Robert. 'Nothing in the whole outfit seems to do what it's supposed to. I wish I'd never seen the thing.'

In vain had Robert tried to lose his conjuring set. He had left it on buses and on trains but always someone had found it and kindly pursued him with it. In any case it wouldn't have been any good, because Roxana would only have got him another.

'Now, Robert dear, don't be childish,' said Roxana with a maternal smile. 'All conjurers make little mistakes sometimes. They just cover them up with patter.'

'Patter!' echoed the goaded Robert. 'I can't patter. I'm just no good at pattering. I keep telling you, Roxana, I *can't* patter. I never know what to say. I can't make speeches of any sort. I've never been able to. I always get out of them at rugger and tennis dinners and things like that. The minute I stand up with everyone looking at me I turn into a jibbering idiot – only I can't even jibber. I just grin and go hot and cold. Patter!' he ended helplessly.

Roxana smiled again. There was obstinacy in the curves of her exquisite mouth. She had determined that Robert should do this and nothing would make her change her mind.

'Well, darling, I've explained how it is,' she said. 'We feel that we ought to give Egerton a party, but Mother doesn't want a lot of rough boys rampaging over the house, so we've asked Mrs Lane's brother – a charming man who's lived abroad a lot, you know – to entertain them for half an hour by a little talk on his experiences, and all you have to do is to entertain them by a few conjuring tricks for half an hour after that. *Surely* you can do tricks and patter for just half an hour, Robert. It's no time at all.'

'It's a lifetime,' said Robert. 'It'll turn me into an old man. It's nearly turned me into one already. When I tried the wretched things again last night, I was surprised to see that my hair wasn't white by the time I'd finished.'

'But you've got the glove puppet, dear, haven't you?'

Robert gave a hollow laugh.

'That thing! Yes.'

'Robert dear, don't be so difficult. It's a most amusing little glove puppet . . . Uncle Marmaduke made us *die* of laughing with it at our Christmas party. He did a few conjuring tricks – they turned out quite well, so I don't see why yours shouldn't – then he said, "Now I'm going to hand the show over to an old friend of mine", and he brought out the glove puppet and made it talk to him and do – well – do a lot of funny things, you know, and we *died* of laughter.'

'Why can't he do it now?' said Robert.

'I told you, dear. He's somewhere in the Mexican Gulf.'

'Serve him right!' said Robert.

'On a job, I mean . . . You've tried it, haven't you? The glove puppet, I mean. You've practised with it?'

Robert thought of the glove puppet – its fatuous idiotic face, its imbecile grin, the gleam of malice in its fixed glass eyes – and groaned.

'I can't *do* anything with the thing,' he said. 'It just sits on my finger like a stuffed bird.'

'Now, dear, don't take such a gloomy view of everything,' said Roxana. 'I think that all performers get a little depressed before the performance, but everything always goes off all right on the night. I'm sure you'll do it perfectly and I shall be very proud of you. It's all so simple darling. You just do your conjuring tricks and cover up any mistakes with patter and then say. "Now I'm handing the show over to an old friend of mine" and take out the glove puppet and – well, do funny things with it and make them laugh.'

'I bet I'll do that all right,' said Robert bitterly.

'It'll soon be over,' Roxana consoled him, 'and next Sunday, you know, we're going out to Mereham Ponds on your motor bike.'

'You really will come, won't you, Roxana?' said Robert.

'Of course, dear. I said I would and I always keep my word. That's why I can't bear the thought of your breaking your word over this conjuring business. Such a little thing to do to please me!'

'And you've not forgotten that you're coming to the dinner and dance in Hadley with me, have you, Roxana?'

'Of course not, dear.'

'It's a marvellous floor, you know,' said Robert, brightening.

'Yes, and I hear they're having a dance band from London . . . I thought I'd wear my cherry-coloured dress. You do like me in it, don't you, Robert?'

'*Like* you!' stammered Robert. 'You look adorable in it, Roxana. You look . . . you look . . .'

The conversation began to run on more cheerful lines.

William and Ginger had reached Lilac Cottage and were standing at the gate, watching a short dark man who had just emerged from it and was hurrying down the road.

'It's that foreign man that's just come to live there,' said William. 'He calls himself Mr Jones, but he's foreign really . . . I say, Ginger!'

'Yes?'

'He lives there alone an' he's gone out an' left the door open. Let's pretend to be burglars an' go in. It'll make a jolly good crime.'

'Gosh, William!' said Ginger aghast. 'You can't do a *real* crime.'

''S not much of a crime, jus' goin' into someone's house,' said William. 'If we're goin' to train Jumble for a p'lice dog, we've *got* to give him a crime to practise on. It's not fair to him not to. I bet the p'lice do all sorts of crimes – murder an' everythin' else – when they're trainin' their p'lice dogs. We can't do any harm jus' goin' into someone's house. I bet Jumble'll smell us out an' come along in no time. He'd be jolly disappointed if he found us not doin' a crime.'

'Yes, but listen, William,' said Ginger. 'I still don't think we ought to. I still think—'

But William had already made his way down the path and was entering the open front door. Ginger followed, torn between apprehension and excitement.

They looked round the small narrow hall. A hat and coat hung on the hatstand. An ancient suitcase was balanced on a chair.

'Nothin' worth stealin' here,' said William.

'Gosh, William!' protested Ginger again. 'You can't axshully *steal* anythin'.'

But he spoke without conviction. William, having embarked on a role, was apt to be carried away by it. He was now a criminal with a police dog hot on his tracks. There was no time to be lost. He must act quickly. Already he was entering a room that led off the hall. It was furnished sparsely as a living-room. William threw a quick frowning glance round it.

'Nothin' worth stealin' there, either,' he said.

He entered the kitchen.

'Nothin' there either,' he said.

Ginger drew a breath of relief.

'Come on, then. Let's get out quick,' he said.

'I've got to find somethin' to steal first,' said William irritably. 'I'm a crim'nal, aren't I? I've broke into someone's house to steal somethin', haven't I? Well, then, I've got to steal somethin'. Stands to reason. Ole Jumble'd be mad if he'd taken all that trouble learnin' to track crim'nals an' then found there wasn't a crim'nal to track.

It'd put him against bein' a p'lice dog for the rest of his life . . .'

He returned to the hall and opened the suitcase. It held a pair of pyjamas, a dressing-gown, shaving outfit, bedroom slippers, and a large unwieldy looking torch. William took out the torch and pressed the button.

'Doesn't work,' he said. 'Listen. I've got to steal somethin' so I'll steal this ole torch. It doesn't work anyway, so no one'll miss it.'

'Not *really* steal it?' said Ginger.

'No, I s'pose not,' said William, coming reluctantly down to earth. 'No, I s'pose not really. I'll put it in my pocket an' pretend to steal it, jus' to give Jumble a bit of a crime to find when he comes along. Can't think why he hasn't come along by now. Look out of the window, Ginger, an' see if he's comin'.'

'I'LL PUT IT IN MY POCKET AND PRETEND TO STEAL IT,'
SAID WILLIAM.

Ginger looked out of the window.

'No, but – gosh, William, the man is! Mr Jones. The foreigner. He's comin' back.'

'All right,' said William tersely. 'Let's get out quick.'

They slipped out of the open door and scrambled through the hedge, looking apprehensively at the swarthy little man who was making his way towards them. Mr Jones, however, was both short-sighted and absent-minded. He did not even notice the two small boys who walked past him in silence with set expressionless faces, their eyes fixed on the distant horizon.

Once past him, they relaxed.

'We were only just in time,' said Ginger.

'I can't think why Jumble hasn't come,' said William, whose mind was still set on the main purpose of the expedition. 'We took all that trouble bein' crim'nals an' he jus' didn't turn up . . . P'r'aps,' he added, unwilling to admit any flaw in his trainee, 'he's found a bigger crime somewhere else. He may've caught a murderer or some-thin'.'

'We'll prob'ly meet him on the way,' said Ginger. 'He may've got into a muddle about what sort of dog he's s'posed to be. He's only jus' finished bein' a regimental mascot an' he was a husky before that.'

They made their way across the fields. There was no sign of Jumble. Henry and Douglas were waiting for them in the old barn.

'Did he find you?' said Henry.

'He never came at all,' said William. 'When did you let him go?'

'We let him go soon after you'd gone. He took your cap. We thought he'd gone after you.'

'Wonder what's happened to him,' said William, his face tense with anxiety.

'P'r'aps he thought you were trainin' him to be a lost dog,' suggested Douglas.

'Oh, shut up,' said William. 'Come on. Let's go'n' look for him.'

But an exhaustive search of the countryside still revealed no trace of Jumble.

'I bet he's been stolen,' said William despondently. 'I bet someone saw him doin' those tricks we taught him an' wants to have him in a show. Those Bertram Mills people, I shouldn't wonder.'

'Well, what can we do about it now?' said Ginger.

'I'm goin' to the p'lice station,' said William with an air of decision. 'I'm goin' to tell them that a valu'ble performing dog's been lost an' that they've got to find it.'

'You ought to offer a reward,' said Henry. 'That's what they do. They offer a reward.'

'Well, I'll offer a reward, then,' said William. 'Anyone that finds him can have six of my marbles an' my king conker an' those liquorice bootlaces we bought this mornin'.'

'We've eaten 'em all,' Ginger reminded him.

'So we have,' said William. 'Well, they can have my one an' sixpenny bus ticket an' my tame caterpillar. That makes a jolly good reward. Now come on.'

Still wearing his air of stern decision, William led his band down the road and into the police station. The air of stern decision turned to one of surprise as his eye fell on the only other occupant of the room – the swarthy little man whom they had last seen making his way towards Lilac Cottage. He had bright black eyes, thick bushy eyebrows and outstanding ears, and he was tapping his foot impatiently on the floor. He threw the Outlaws a glance that was without recognition or interest and continued to tap his foot impatiently on the floor, his eyes fixed expectantly on a closed door.

Suddenly the door opened and the red-haired policeman appeared, carrying a note-book.

'Now, Mr Jones,' he said, 'let's have details of this theft.'

'My suitcase,' said Mr Jones with a sweeping gesture. 'Eet has been stolen. Eet has been pinched.'

'Suitcase,' wrote the policeman in his note-book then turned to the Outlaws. 'What do you kids want?'

'We've had a valu'ble dog stolen,' said William with dignity. ''Least, we've got a valu'ble dog missing. It's a jolly intelligent dog an'—'

'No stray dogs reported that I know of,' said the policeman shortly, 'so clear out.' He turned again to Mr Jones. 'What was in the suitcase?' The Outlaws hovered, listening in the doorway. The policeman decided to ignore them and get on with the business in hand. 'Can you give me a list of the contents?'

Again the little man flung out his arms in an expansive gesture.

'Ah, ze contents . . . ze articles of ze toilet, zey matter not . . . ze pyjams, as you say, zey matter not . . . ze brosh of hair, ze comb of hair, zey matter not . . . ze soap of shave, ze raze of shave, zey matter not . . . ze gown of dressing, eet matters not . . .'

'Well, let's get on to what does matter,' said the policeman impatiently.

'Ze papers,' said the little man, mysteriously. 'Ze papers of importance.'

'Ah!' said the policeman, his spirits rising as he saw himself unmasking an underground organisation of communist activities and even bringing to light some missing diplomats. 'Papers of importance . . . Political, I take it?'

'No, no,' said the little man, waving his arms round like the sails of a windmill. 'Papers of ze profession.'

'Profession? What profession?' said the policeman, sucking the point of his pencil with an air of mystification.

'Ze clown,' said the little man.

'What clown?' said the policeman helplessly.

The little man described a circle in the air with his hand then dealt himself a resounding blow on the chest.

'Me,' he said proudly. 'Me, ze clown. In ze old days. In Budapest. Before ze Iron Curtain drop. I was zere at the top of ze tree of ze clowning. I have clowned to Royalty itself. Millions have seen me, have split open their sides, as you say, with ze laughing.'

'Yes, but—' began the policeman.

The little man, however, having got into his stride, was not so easily checked.

'Zen ze Iron Curtain, eet drop. I flee, but I take wiz me my most precious papers, ze what you call ze handbills, ze notices cut from ze newspapers zat proclaim me as ze tree tops of ze clowning. I give up ze clowning, but ze memory, eet is ze joy, ze pride, ze comfortableness. When ze sadness comes over me I take ze papers from their hiding-place and I live again ze triumph. In my mind I leap, I gambol, I doze treeks. I hear ze laughter, ze clapping, ze roars of ze multitudes.'

'Well, now, Mr Jones,' said the policeman, looking at him with interest, 'we never knew you were a clown.'

'MILLIONS HAVE SEEN ME, HAVE SPLIT OPEN THEIR SIDES WITH ZE
LAUGHING,' SAID THE LITTLE MAN.

'No, no,' said the little man. 'I come to England. I am –
how you say – naturalised like ze daffodils in ze adver-
tisements. I give up my Hungarian name. I take ze grand
old English name of Mr Jones. I make myself ze serious
English country gentleman. I plant ze onions and ze
rhubarb in my garden. I eat ze roast beef, ze fish and
cheeps, ze sausage and mash – no longer ze goulash. I
gaze on ze game of ze cricket. I go to ze fête in the garden
of ze house of ze vicar. Almost – but not quite – I learn ze
golf. I throw my fling into ze pools of ze football. I—'

'Now listen, Mr Jones,'said the policeman firmly. 'All
this isn't leading us nowhere. Let's get back to the suitcase. Where was the suitcase?' He threw a harassed

glance towards the door. 'I thought I'd told you kids to clear out.'

The Outlaws edged a few inches further away and still hovered there listening.

'In ze hall of ze house.' said Mr Jones, 'standing ready for ze departure. I arrange to stay for ze end of ze week wiz an old Hungarian comrade in London. I pack ze case. I remember that I must put a letter to ze post. I go to ze box pillar. I leave ze door open for so short a journey. I put ze letter in ze box pillar. I return. Ze suitcase, eet is still there when I return. Zen I remember too that I need more of ze paste for ze teeth. I hurry myself to ze village, to buy myself more of ze paste for ze teeth. Again I leave ze door open—'

'Ah,' said the policeman as if at last finding something to hold on to. 'You left the door open.'

'Only a moment was it in my mind to be out of ze house, but I wait in ze shop while ze customer and ze shopkeeper talk of ze weather and ze rheumatism and ze tomatoes of ze outdoors . . . zen I return to find my suitcase gone. I am unable to believe my sense. My very blood, eet stand on end. My—'

'Yes, yes,' said the policeman soothingly. 'Must have been a nasty shock. May've been some of those fruit pickers. They're supposed to have done a lot of petty thefts round here lately. Your open door must have tempted them and when they saw the suitcase . . .'

'No, no,' said the little man, waving his arms again excitedly. 'Eet was some enemy, someone jealous of my fame, my professional repute. In ze days before ze Iron Curtain drop I had on all sides ze jealous enemies. Zey follow me. Zey steal ze papers zat are to be ze consolationing of my old age, ze precious memories of my life on ze treetops of ze clowning.'

'Come, come!' said the policeman. 'That's a bit far-fetched. These papers were loose in your suitcase, you say?'

'Not loose. No, no! Never loose. I hide zem. I conceal zem with cunning. I hide zem where no thief, no enemy would ever sink of looking – in an old – what you call torch lighter. And I pack eet in my suitcase because eet go wherever I go. It ees my past, my history, my—'

'Yes, yes, yes,' interrupted the policeman. 'Now let's try and get it all straight. What time did you leave the house?' He turned to the door again. 'Will you kids—'

But the Outlaws had vanished and were already walking down the road. William's face wore a frozen look of horror.

'Gosh, Ginger! Those papers mus' have been in that torch I did my crime on.'

'Yes. Where is it?' said Ginger.

'Dunno,' said William, 'I put it in my pocket an' I never thought of it again after you saw him comin' along.' He dug his hands into his pockets. 'It's not there now . . . Come on. Let's see if I left it in the old barn.'

They hurried again across the fields to the old barn.

'Yes! There it is!' said William, picking up the torch from a dark corner. 'I mus' have put it there without thinkin' or it mus' have fallen out of my pocket.' He took off the cap of the torch and drew out a roll of faded hand-bills and yellowed newspaper cuttings. 'Yes, that's it, all right.' He packed them carefully back. 'Gosh! Now we've got to go an' give them to him. He'll be mad.'

But Mr Jones was not mad. Standing at his front door, he watched with a puzzled frown the four boys who marched slowly in single file up his garden path . . . then, suddenly noticing the torch in William's hand, flung his arms about him and kissed him on both cheeks.

'Ah, ze hero! Ze brave boy! He hears of my loss. He has noted ze thief carrying ze suitcase. He runs after him. He – what you call – tackles him. He – what you call – gives him ze bashing. He takes from him my torch lighter with its precious contents. He knows that ze pyjams, ze raze of shave, ze slippers of ze bedroom matter not. It is

MR JONES FLUNG HIS ARMS ROUND WILLIAM AND KISSED HIM.

ze torch lighter he demands. At ze risk of his life he secures ze precious torch lighter. He brings eet to me. Ze brave young hero!'

He approached William again with outstretched arms and William, whose feelings at the first embrace would have defied description, backed hastily upon Ginger, causing momentary confusion in the ranks behind him. Douglas picked himself up from the ground and looked longingly at the gate.

'Come on. Let's go now,' he said.

But William, having evaded the outstretched arms, was making a gallant effort to explain the situation.

'You see, we wanted to train him for a p'lice dog, so we'd got to c'mit a crime to get him trained.'

The others hastened to his support.

'We'd tried a greyhound.'

'An' a St Bernard.'

'He was a jolly good St Bernard, but he couldn't keep in practise 'cause the snow kept meltin'.'

'He wasn't much good as a reg'mental mascot or a husky.'

'Anyway, I took your torch for the crime 'cause I thought it didn't look much good. An' I didn't mean axshully to take it away. I sort of put it in my pocket an' forgot it.'

'He was gettin' a bit anxious about Jumble.'

'Can't think what's happened to him. He gen'rally stays with us all the time.'

'Well, he's missed his chance of bein' a p'lice dog now.'

'We don't know anythin' about the suitcase.'

'I jus' took the torch out of the suitcase for my crime an' went away. The suitcase was all right then.'

'He started off in the right direction an' he took William's cap with him.'

'I'm sorry about it,' ended William. 'We brought it back quick as we could.'

But this account of the true state of affairs only seemed to increase the little man's gratitude.

'Ah, but if you had not taken it for ze crime, as you say, for ze training of your p'lice dog, it would have remained in ze suitcase and ze villian would now have it in his possession. For ze suitcase, for ze articles of toilet, I do not care. Ze stealing insurance will pay for zem, but nozing – nozing in ze world – would have paid for my precious treasure that you have so nobly returned to me.' He beamed again at William and again William backed apprehensively. 'If eet is in my power to reward you, if zere is anything that you would like that I could geeve you or do for you . . .'

William's countenance remained gloomy and overcast. The only thing in the world he wanted was the return of Jumble. So entirely did this anxiety fill his mind that there was room for nothing else.

Suddenly he saw Hubert Lane passing the gate. Hubert stopped, grinned at them with malicious triumph, gave a gloating laugh and again ran off as fast as his fat legs could carry him. That recalled to William the other anxiety which hung like a dark cloud at the back of his mind. He looked at Mr Jones and a light broke gradually through his gloom.

'Well, there's one thing,' he said. 'There's one thing that . . . Gosh! If you'd do it!'

'Tell me,' said Mr Jones.

William told him. The little man listened and shook his head regretfully.

'I am afraid not . . . No, I am afraid it ees not possible . . . Ze equipment . . . Yes, I have ze equipment, but no . . . It ees years since I practise myself . . . I will sink about it. I promise I will sink . . . but no, I am afraid not.'

Lunch at the Brown's that day was a silent meal. Only Mrs Brown, Robert and William partook of it, and both Robert and William were plunged so deep in melancholy that Mrs Brown's most determined attempts to cheer them met with no response.

'Gosh! If he's been run over . . .' said William mournfully.

'I'm sure he hasn't, dear,' Mrs Brown reassured him. 'He never has been yet and there's no reason why he should be today.'

'Yes, there is,' said William. 'He's never stayed away as long as this before. I've been lookin' for him all morning and I've not found him. I'm goin' to look for him all afternoon.'

'You must go to the party this afternoon, you know, dear.'

'Gosh!' said William, outraged. 'I can't go to an ole party with Jumble lost.'

'You must, dear,' said Mrs Brown firmly. 'If Jumble comes back while you're away I'll ring up and send you a message, but you've accepted the invitation to the party and you must go to it.'

A groan escaped Robert at the mention of the party.

'Now cheer up, William dear,' went on Mrs Brown, 'and have some of this nice apple pudding.'

'No, thank you,' said William. 'I've got a funny feeling

in my stomach with Jumble being lost an' it stops me wantin' to eat.'

Robert looked at his young brother with a gleam of hope. It was unprecedented for William to refuse apple pudding.

'Perhaps he's got something infectious,' he said. 'If he has I don't think I ought to go. It wouldn't be fair on the others.'

'No, of course he hasn't,' said Mrs Brown, adding, with an optimism that was little short of heroic, 'Jumble will turn up and Robert's little tricks at the party will go off splendidly and you'll both have a lovely time and – and everything will be all right.'

Robert gave the remark the tribute of his hollow laugh as he rose with mournful dignity from the table.

The two set off from the Brown's house later in the afternoon, both spruced and neat in party attire, both still enveloped in a cloud of despondency. They walked side by side in silence, their shoulders hunched, their eyes bent on the ground. Their common misery seemed to bridge the gulf that usually divided them.

'I'm sure he'll turn up all right, old chap,' said Robert.

'Thanks,' said William gruffly, and, not to be outdone, added, 'an' I'm sure your conjuring tricks'll go off all right.'

Robert's 'Thanks' was more like a moan.

Their funereal progress made the walk take longer than it usually took, and the party was already assembled when they reached Roxana's house. Hubert's uncle was there – a stout pompous little man with an upstanding quiff of grey hair like a cockatoo's crest.

'Quick!' said Roxana's mother to him. 'Before they get rough!'

She knew William's reputation and had eyed him apprehensively as he entered the room, but the idea of 'roughness' was incompatible with the drooping figure that confronted her.

'I'm expectin' an important telephone message,' he said to her mysteriously. 'You'll let me know at once when it comes, won't you?'

Then he looked about him. Chairs, already filled by the guests, were ranged in front of the open french windows, where a space had been left for the entertainers. At the back of the room tea was laid on a buffet table. In the middle of the table was a pyramid of cream doughnuts that would ordinarily have made his mouth water, but now he passed them over with a lack-lustre eye.

Egerton greeted his guests with the politeness due from a perfect little gentleman, Hubert sniggered in a corner, William took his seat between Ginger and Robert, and Hubert's uncle strode to the space in front of the window and began his performance.

The audience listened – restive but not wholly unimpressed. Hubert's uncle had collected a large number of heroic exploits from various sources and recounted them in detail, making himself the hero of each and interspersing them with a few jokes at which he laughed so heartily that the audience, led by Hubert, found themselves joining in. Then, beaming, complacent, satisfied, he returned to his seat.

Miserably, fearfully, Robert crept up to the table, spread out his conjuring set and began . . . It was worse than his worst fears. Scarves that were supposed to knot themselves together remained apart. Handkerchiefs that were supposed to change colour stayed the same. Things that – put into tins and boxes – were supposed to change into something else, emerged unaltered.

It was Hubert who started the mocking laughter. It was William and the Outlaws who started a counter action of laughter that, though a little unnatural, was obviously intended to be sincere.

'He's bein' funny,' whispered William to those around him. 'It's jolly clever. It's much harder to make 'em come out like that than to do it prop'ly.'

Roxana watched with a frozen smile and a look that boded little good to the performer. Egerton applauded mechanically at the end of each ghastly failure.

'And now,' said Robert at last in a voice that was hoarse with despair, 'I'm going to hand the show over to an old friend of mine.'

He was just feeling in his pockets for the puppet and realising with nightmare horror that he'd left it behind . . . when a cloaked figure suddenly appeared at the open french window behind him. It stood there for a few moments then flung off the cloak and entered the room. It was Mr Jones, but an unrecognisable Mr Jones. He was a clown, with reddened nose, whitened face, clown's costume and hat. Without a second's hesitation he began his performance. He leapt, he gambolled, he cracked jokes, he did tricks. The audience roared with laughter and rocked with delight. Roxana beamed upon Robert, who had taken his seat and sat as if stunned, his mouth hanging open in amazement. Only Hubert and his uncle watched dourly, scowling at performer and performance. The Outlaws yelled exultantly. William was so much entranced that he almost – but not quite – forgot the anxiety about Jumble that tugged at his heart.

The clown did a final series of somersaults round the 'stage', had a final boxing match with himself, getting so comically entangled with himself that the audience almost wept with laughter, performed a final conjuring trick, played a final game of Hide and Seek with one of his legs that he pretended to have lost, then stood in the centre of the stage making his final bow.

And at that moment there appeared at the open window behind him – Jumble.

He was muddy and dishevelled, one ear was bleeding and he carried a sodden shapeless object in his mouth.

When released by Henry and Douglas, Jumble had honestly intended to seek out his master, but, passing Jenks's farm, he found a rat hunt in progress and stopped to join in. Exhilarated by the experience, and still harbouring dark suspicions that another bout of 'training' was in store for him, he had decided to take the day off and had gone rabbiting in Marleigh Woods. Through all the vicissitudes of the day, however, he had never entirely forgotten William's cap. He had left it in hedges and ditches but always he had gone back to retrieve it, and he held it proudly in his mouth now as he stood – apologetic

A ROAR OF APPLAUSE BROKE OUT. WILLIAM'S HEART WAS FULL TO BURSTING POINT.

but by no means dissatisfied with himself – looking round the room.

His eye fell on William and he took a flying leap into the room to reach him, catching Mr Jones off his guard, so that the two of them rolled on the floor together. When at last Jumble extricated himself, the clown's hat hung askew over one of his ears.

Mr Jones scrambled to his feet.

'Ze problem solved,' he said. 'He is ze circus dog.'

He took up William's cap, put it on his own head, straightened the clown's hat on Jumble's head, beckoned Robert . . . and the three stood in a row facing the audience, Robert and Mr Jones each holding a paw of Jumble's – Jumble wearing the clown's hat, Mr Jones William's cap, and Robert a look of dazed bewilderment.

A roar of applause broke out. William sat and watched, his heart full to bursting point. Everyone was surging round the trio to congratulate them and shake hands.

'Robert was marvellous, wasn't he? It was the funniest take-off of an amateur conjurer that I've ever seen.'

'It was a *scream*!'

'Yes, and all the time he'd got this other chap to give the real show.'

Hubert's uncle had gone home.

'A crude performance,' he commented dispassionately as he departed.

Hubert sat scowling and muttering to himself.

Roxana clung to Robert's arm, still beaming at him with proud affection.

'Darling,' she said, 'I misjudged you so horribly at one point. I didn't realise that you were trying to be funny.'

Robert, who still felt that the whole world was wheeling round him in circles, blinked and murmured:

'That's quite all right, dear. Don't give it another thought.'

William watched and listened with waning interest.

The shouting and the tumult had died. The excitement was over. Jumble had been found. Robert had not disgraced himself or the family. His mind, eased of its burden, could now turn itself to more important matters.

Unobtrusively but in a business-like fashion, he edged his way to the buffet table and set to work on the cream doughnuts.

Chapter 4

Don William and the Sun-Bather

'What's a stone's throw?' said Ginger.

'What d'you mean, what's a stone's throw?' said William.

The two were walking down the Marleigh road, Jumble trotting at their heels with an air of sedateness that he shed occasionally to plunge into the hedge after a sparrow or into the ditch after an imaginary rat.

'Well, my aunt's goin' to live in a new house an' the estate agent said it was a stone's throw from the shops.'

William picked up a stone.

'I'll show you what a stone's throw is,' he said.

He meant to throw the stone along the road but Jumble, taking the action as an invitation to a game, leapt up exuberantly and flung him off his balance.

The stone soared over the hedge into the garden they were passing.

There came the sinister sound of breaking glass.

'Gosh!' said William with horror. 'Let's get off quick before—'

But at that moment a woman's face appeared over the

hedge. It did not wear the expression that William was accustomed to see on the faces of people whose property he had damaged. It was a round, elderly, cheerful face with kindly blue eyes and untidy grey hair. A smile broke out over it as the blue eyes fell on William and Ginger.

'Oh, it's you, is it?' she said. 'I couldn't think what it was.'

'I'm sorry if we've brok'n anything,' said William hoarsely.

'Only the garden frame,' said the woman carelessly, 'and it was broken already and we never use it, anyway. Come in and see for yourselves.'

She opened a gate in the hedge. William and Ginger entered.

It was a large garden, untended and overgrown. A garden frame with most of its panes missing stood near the gate-post. Weeds choked the patches of ground that had obviously once been vegetable plots. A derelict greenhouse sagged against the wall that ran down the side of the garden.

They stood looking around them.

'Yes, it's dreadful, isn't it?' said the woman, smiling.

'Would you like us to tidy it up for you?' said William.

He felt grateful to the woman for her calm acceptance of his stone, and gratitude with William was an emotion that called for immediate outlet.

'Oh, no, thank you,' said the woman. 'It's past hope, and, anyway, we're removing soon. I only came down to try to find some cress for sandwiches for tea. There doesn't seem to be any . . . We're in a terrible muddle, of course, with this removal hanging over us.'

'Well, can we do something to help?' said William.

'We'd like to help 'cause of you bein' so decent about that stone.'

The woman laughed.

'Well, actually, I'm dusting books at the moment. Would you like to help with that?'

'Yes,' said William.

Dusting books was not one of William's favourite occupations but the untended garden, the large gaunt house that stood at the end of it and the vague pleasant woman who was its mistress interested him.

'And what about your friend?' said the woman. 'Would he like to come, too?'

'Yes, I s'pect he would, wouldn't you, Ginger?' said William.

'Yes, please,' said Ginger.

There was a faint note of apprehension in Ginger's voice. It all seemed simple and straightforward enough so far, but with William in charge things were apt to get out of hand without even a moment's notice.

William turned to look at Jumble, who was busy uprooting an overgrown purple sprouting broccoli.

'You don't mind Jumble comin' too, do you?' he said. 'He won't be a nuisance. 'Least, he'll try not to be.'

'Oh, yes, let him come,' said the woman. 'There's nothing he could harm, anyway . . . My name's Miss Granter.' She led the way through the jungle of weeds. 'It's a disgrace, isn't it? When I was a girl it was all beautifully kept up, of course, with gardeners and orchids in the greenhouse and not a weed to be seen and even peaches against the wall, but' – she shrugged – 'times have changed. There's only my sister and myself left now and we can't afford gardeners and my sister's an invalid and – well, there just isn't the money to keep the place up, so we're moving out of it.'

They entered the side door and passed through a large bare hall into a spacious room lined with bookcases.

'This was my father's library in the old days,' said Miss Granter, 'and these are his books. He was a scholar, so they're all very dull. I've never read any of them. I prefer thrillers . . . Now here are two dusters and you can reach the higher ones with this broom. Just flick them over. Don't bother to take them out . . . Wait a minute. I've got some raspberry buns in the oven. They should be ready by now. Would you like one?'

'Yes, please,' said William and Ginger simultaneously and Jumble pricked up his ears and stopped chasing a small squat footstool round the room.

Miss Granter went out and returned a few moments later with a plate of raspberry buns. They were large and warm and succulent-looking, generously laced with raspberry jam.

'Now sit down and try them,' she said, 'and I'll tell you all about it.'

They sat down cross-legged on the floor with the plate of raspberry buns in front of them and got to work.

'They're jolly good,' said Ginger.

'Yes, they jolly well are,' agreed William, breaking off a small piece of his bun and putting it into Jumble's eager thrusting mouth. He glanced round the book shelves. 'Why are you botherin' to dust them if you're removing?'

'That's what I was going to tell you,' said Miss Granter, flicking the books with a long-handled feather duster. 'You see, my sister and I are moving because the house is mortgaged up to the hilt and we haven't the money to keep it up and the removal will take all our spare cash and my sister's been very ill and the doctor says she ought to have a holiday, so I decided to sell my father's library – we don't want it – and take the holiday with the proceeds. A man's coming down from a London firm this afternoon to look at it, so I thought I'd just – freshen them up with a duster, as it were, to make them look better. They were all good books in their time. They ought to fetch a good price. It will do my poor sister such a lot of good to get a holiday. As a matter of fact, we've neither of us had a holiday for ten years.'

The door opened and another woman entered. She looked pale and worn and fragile. She threw a nervous glance round the room.

'This is my sister,' said Miss Granter cheerfully. 'These kind boys are helping me dust the books, Erica dear.' William and Ginger disposed of the last crumbs of the raspberry buns and set to work with duster and broom. 'It occurred to me that they might fetch a better price if we got the dust off.'

'I thought I'd sit here,' said Miss Erica in a gentle ghost-like voice, 'then I can see when the man arrives.'

'Yes, dear.'

'Torquay would be lovely, wouldn't it, Lucy? Do you think we could manage Torquay.'

'I'm sure we could, dear. I was just telling these boys about it. Father was very proud of his library. It ought to be worth quite a lot of money.'

'We went to Torquay once when we were children, didn't we? I keep thinking about it. I keep saying to myself, "Perhaps in two weeks' time we'll be in Torquay". It sounds silly, doesn't it, but I've got a sort of *hunger* for the sea. It's just the thought of the holiday that keeps me going.'

'Yes, dear,' said Miss Granter soothingly. 'Now you mustn't worry. Everything's going to be all right.'

Miss Erica had lowered herself into an arm-chair by the window. She leant forward, her thin form tensed, her eyes fixed on the gate.

'What time is the man coming?'

'He should be here any moment now, dear. I've got him a wonderful tea to put him into a good temper. I've got cucumber sandwiches and tomato sandwiches – I'd meant to make cress sandwiches, too, but the cress seems to have vanished – and raspberry buns and one of my sponges.'

'It sounds lovely,' said Miss Erica. She looked down at Jumble, who was sitting by her side, gazing up at her soulfully. Jumble had a strong sense of the dramatic and liked to pose as the Faithful Hound in suitable circumstances. 'A nice dog . . . Where has it come from?'

'These boys brought it.'

'A very nice dog.' Jumble laid his head on her knee, intensifying his Faithful Hound expression. Suddenly Miss Erica's frail form stiffened and she gave a gasp. 'The man . . . The man's here.'

They all looked out of the window. A plump, dapper little man with a sleek dark moustache and sleek dark hair was opening the gate.

Miss Erica started to her feet.

'I'll leave you, dear,' she said. 'You're the business woman and you'll need all your business acumen to deal with him. I might only distract you if I stayed.'

'Perhaps, dear,' said Miss Granter gently.

Miss Erica left the room and her sister went to the door to admit the visitor.

'Mr Bailey?' she said.

'Yes,' said the visitor.

He had a harsh grating voice and the smile that he flashed round the room as he entered the library was oily and over-pleasant.

'Well, well, well,' he said, putting his attaché case on the table and rubbing his hands. 'Quite a pleasure to come down to the country this time of year. A lovely spot you live in.' He turned to William and Ginger. 'And these little chaps—?'

'Just two friends of mine,' said Miss Granter quietly. 'Now these are the books, Mr Bailey. I'm afraid I don't know much about them. They all belonged to my father. I' – her voice faltered a little – 'I do hope you'll be able to offer me a good price for them.'

Mr Bailey took a pair of spectacles from his pocket, perched them on his nose and began to examine the books. His eyes went swiftly along the shelves. They seemed to linger at a spot on the corner of the second shelf, then passed on quickly, scanning the rows, one after another.

At last he took off his spectacles and turned to Miss Granter. His mouth was pursed, his expression pained and regretful.

'I'm sorry to disappoint you, Miss Granter,' he said, 'but I'm afraid there's nothing here that my firm would care to handle.'

'Oh dear!' said Miss Granter.

She had gone very pale.

'It's all twopence-a-shelf stuff,' said Mr Bailey. 'It

doesn't matter whom you asked down. They'd all tell you the same. And of course we don't handle stuff like that. It wouldn't even cover the carriage.'

'I don't know how I'm going to tell my sister,' said Miss Granter. 'She's counting on it.'

'I'm very sorry,' said Mr Bailey. 'If I could have made you an offer, you may be sure I would have done.'

'Of course,' said Miss Granter. She rallied her scattered forces. 'It's so good of you to have come all this way and I'm sorry for your sake as well as my own that it's been a wasted journey.'

Mr Bailey's teeth fairly glistened as he smiled at her.

'Well, well, well . . . We're supposed to charge our expenses, but I shall be very glad to make an exception in your case. As a matter of fact, I meant to bring a book with me to read in the train – I always feel lost without a book to read in the train – so I suggest that instead of paying my expenses you give me one of your books to read in the train.'

'Of course,' agreed Miss Granter. 'That's very generous of you. Take any you like.'

Again Mr Bailey's eyes seemed to rove idly along the shelves coming to rest again at the end of the second shelf.

'Ah, there's my old friend, Don Quixote,' he said. 'How I used to love those stories as a boy! I think I'd like to re-read them. I always enjoy re-reading old favourites on a train journey.' He took out the book and turned over the pages. 'Our old friend, Don Quixote with his stout little esquire Sancho Panza and his steed Rosinante. He wasn't very fortunate in his adventures.'

'No,' said Miss Granter earnestly, 'but he had the courage to face and fight evil-doers. I only wish we had a few Don Quixotes in these lax days. These waves of crime sweep over the country unchecked. People have lost the spirit of the knights of old. They've grown lethargic and indifferent. They no longer face and fight evildoers. They pass them by with a shrug.'

'Quite, quite,' said Mr Bailey. His eyes returned to the shelves. 'There appear to be four volumes. Perhaps . . .'

'Oh certainly, take them,' said Miss Granter. 'I'm only too pleased for you to have them.'

'TAKE THEM,' SAID MISS GRANTER. 'I'M ONLY TOO PLEASED FOR YOU TO HAVE THEM.'

Mr Bailey slipped the books into his case beneath an accumulation of papers, maps and miscellaneous objects.

'And now I think I must be getting on my way.'

'Oh, but you must stay for tea.'

'No, no, no, thank you, but I can't stay to tea.' A touch of nervousness had invaded Mr Bailey's manner. 'I'm afraid I must be getting on.'

'But there's no train back to London before the five-forty-five . . . Oh, you *must* stay to tea.'

Mr Bailey's small eyes darted round as if in search of escape. Then he submitted with another glistening smile.

'Oh, well . . . thank you very much.'

'And we won't tell my sister about the books, if you don't mind. Not just for the present. We'll pretend that you've not quite finished the valuing. I'll break it to her later when you've gone.' They went to the door. She turned to look at William and Ginger. 'Would you boys care to stay to tea?'

'No, thank you,' said William.

She went from the room with her escort and they heard the closing of the dining-room door.

'She won't get that holiday,' said Ginger. 'I didn't like him, did you?'

'Gosh, no!' said William, 'but we can't do anythin' about it.'

There were adult problems that William occasionally tried to solve but there were others that he recognised as beyond his powers. This one he recognised as beyond his powers. He put it out of his mind.

'It was rather int'restin' about that Don Quixote man,' he said. He was silent for a few moments, then, 'I *say*, Ginger!'

'Yes?'

'She said they needed a few of them these days. Let's be one. I mean, I'll be him an' you be that Sancho esquire an' Jumble can be Rosinante. We'll go out seekin' for adventures an' evil-doers same as what she said. Gosh! It's *days* – it's nearly *weeks* – since we had an adventure. Let's go out an' find one.'

'We don't know how to do it,' objected Ginger.

'We can find out. Let's have a look at the books. The man won't mind. We won't do them any harm.'

William opened the attaché case and took out the books from beneath the papers.

At this moment Jumble, suffering a sudden reaction from his Faithful Hound act, seized a small hearth brush from the fireplace and began to worry it, chewing the handle, tearing at the bristles, throwing it into the air with little growls of mock ferocity.

'Gosh!' said William. 'Once he gets into that mood there's no stopping him. He'll be startin' on the cushions next. Let's go . . . We'll take the books to the old barn an' have a look at them prop'ly.'

'I dunno that we ought to do that,' said Ginger. 'He wants them to read in the train.'

'He's not goin' till the five-forty-five,' said William. 'We'll have heaps of time to bring them back before then. It won't take us a minute to look through them.'

Jumble was intensifying his attack on the hearth brush and William, with a 'Hi! Boy!' hurried out of the door, followed by Ginger and Jumble – Jumble turning to throw a farewell growl at his half-worried brush.

They crossed the fields to the old barn, sat down on the

ground and opened one of the books. William turned the pages, his bewilderment increasing as he tried to read the seventeenth-century English.

'Having given his horfe a name so much to his fatisfaction he refolved to give himself one.'

'Gosh!' said William. 'The man that wrote that can't spell any better than me. Ole Frenchie'd go for him if he tried it on at school. Look! He can't even spell "horse". Spelling "horse" with an f! Gosh! he mus' be ign'rant.'

As he turned over more pages his bewilderment and disapproval increased.

'Look at this, Ginger. "Confider, fir," answered Sancho, "that thofe, which appear yonder, are not giants but windmills and what feem to be arms are fails which make the millftones go.". . ."One may eafily fee," answered Don Quixote—' He closed the book. 'Gosh! Fancy an ign'rant man like that tryin' to write a book! Whenever he can't spell a word he puts f's all over it. Can't even spell "seem" an' "sail". He can't write English at all. Gosh! he wouldn't get it printed if he tried it on nowadays.' He put the book carelessly on the ground. 'I bet we can find an adventure all right without botherin' with this . . . I'll be Don William an' you be Sancho Ginger an' Jumble can be Rosinante an' we'll set off an' find an adventure an' hunt down evil-doers an' – an' face an' fight 'em, same as she said.'

'I don't see how Jumble can be a horse,' objected Ginger. 'You can't ride him.'

'No, but I can lead him,' said William. 'I bet those knights often led their horses. It mus' have been jolly tirin' for the horses carrying those great tin suits of armour an' I bet the knights often got off to give them a rest . . . Come on, Jumble. I mean, Rosinante.'

He took a piece of string from his pocket, fastened one end to Jumble's collar and proceeded to lead him out of the barn and down the field. Jumble objected to this mode of progression, pulling back with all his might, trying to bite through his 'rein', and finally being dragged along by William, his four paws planted firmly on the ground in an attitude of passionate protest. By the time they had reached the road, however, he had resigned himself to his role and, still upheld by his sense of the dramatic, trailed along at the end of his string, head and tail downcast, with an air of unutterable gloom.

'Now we've got to do it prop'ly,' said William. 'You call me Don William an' I'll call you Sancho Ginger . . . Now keep your eyes open for evil-doers, Sancho Ginger. Come on, Rosinante.'

Jumble, recovering something of his spirit, gave a sudden pull at his string in an ineffectual effort to jerk it out of William's hand.

'Yes, Don William,' said Ginger, 'but I bet we don't find any.'

'''Course we will, Sancho Ginger,' said William. 'There's mus' be hundreds. What about these waves of crime she talked about? The p'lice are so busy stoppin' people parking their cars that they've no time for evil-doers. I heard a grown-up say that so it must be true.'

A survey of the road, however, seemed to disclose no evil-doers. A few old men working in cottage gardens, a few women talking over hedges . . .

'I bet they're all evil-doers really, Sancho Ginger,' said William darkly, 'but they're so cunnin' they're pretendin' not to be. I bet those old men are digging places to hide their loot in an' those women are gettin' foreign secrets out of each other.'

'Well, we can't prove it,' said Ginger.

Ginger was beginning to tire of the expedition and was looking round for some diversion to vary its monotony.

'I bet I could vault that gate, Don William,' he said, looking at a gate that led into a field bordering the road.

'They didn't waste time vaulting gates,' said William a little uncertainly.

'It'll be practice,' urged Ginger. 'We might have to vault one when we're facin' an' fightin' evil-doers.'

'All right,' said William, yielding to temptation.

They approached the gate. Colonel Masters and Mr Saunders – the one large and shaggy, the other small and spare – whom William knew by sight as prominent local figures, stood near it on the road talking.

'We've got to do something about Honiton of The Willows,' Colonel Masters was saying.

'I agree,' said Mr Saunders. 'I'm keeping an eye on him. He just sits pretty.'

'Yes . . . on the fence.'

'People like that are a public danger.'

'Come on,' said William in a quick undertone to Ginger.

They went on down the road, dragging with them the reluctant steed, who had just caught sight of an old shoe in the ditch and was anxious to retrieve it.

'Gosh! Did you hear what they said, Sancho Ginger?' said William, standing still and looking back at the two men. 'They said someone called Honiton was a public danger. That means he's an evil-doer.'

'They said he was jus' sitting pretty,' said Ginger.

'That means he's havin' a good time,' explained William. 'I bet he is, too, till someone faces an' fights him.'

'An' somethin' about a fence . . .'

'Yes . . . *Gosh*, Ginger! I mean, Sancho Ginger' – William's voice rose high with excitement – 'I know what *that* is. I read about it in a story last week. It was a jolly good story, too. There was a villain in it that was a fence an' it meant that he was a sort of thief. He didn't axshully *steal* things but he sold things that other people stole. He was a mos' ghastly villain. Gosh! No wonder they said this man called Honiton's a public danger if he's a fence.'

'Why don't Colonel Masters an' Mr Saunders *do* something, then, if they know about it?' said Ginger.

'It's same as what she said,' said William earnestly. 'They've lost the spirit of the knights of old. They don't face an' fight evil-doers any more. They pass 'em by with a shrug . . . Jus' sayin' they were keeping an eye on him! A villain like that! Come on, Sancho Ginger. We've got to face an' fight him.'

'Might be a bit dangerous if he's a *desperate* evil-doer,' said Ginger.

'I bet that Don Quixote didn't worry about that,' said William. 'He jus' went on an' – an' faced an' fought 'em. Come on, Sancho Ginger.'

'All right, Don William,' said Ginger resignedly, adding, 'We don't know where The Willows is, anyway.'

'I bet we can find it,' said William. 'Come on, Rosinante.' He turned a stern look on Jumble, who, enjoying the brief respite, had sat down to scratch his ear. 'An' try an' act a bit more like a *horse*.'

The three went on down the road.

'Gosh!' said William, suddenly stopping short. 'The Willows.'

They stood, looking at the solid Victorian House that bore the name 'The Willows' in Gothic lettering on its gate.

'*That's* where he lives,' said William. 'We've run him to earth, Sancho Ginger. I bet it's crammed with stolen stuff. Come on.'

'You're not goin' *in*, are you, William?' said Ginger. 'I mean, Don William.'

'Yes, I am. I'm goin' to tie up Rosinante here an' go an' face him an' fight him.'

He tied Jumble's string to the gate-post. Jumble, who had now ceased struggling against fate, lay on the ground, his head between his paws, and settled down to sleep.

'I don't think I'd go *in*, William,' said Ginger, but William was walking slowly and cautiously round the house.

More slowly and more cautiously, Ginger followed. The back door stood ajar. William pushed it open and they entered a large old-fashioned kitchen, spotlessly clean and tidy.

'I bet they're all stolen,' said William, gazing round at the array of pots and pans that stood on the shelves. 'The thieves he sells things for prob'bly made a raid on a saucepan shop last night.'

'They don't look new,' said Ginger.

'No, that's his cunning,' said William. 'This fence I read about made the stuff look diff'rent so's the people he'd stolen it from wouldn't recognise it. He melted silver down . . .' He examined the pallid liquid that half

filled a saucepan on the gas cooker. 'Shouldn't be surprised if that's not melted silver.'

'Smells like chicken soup to me,' said Ginger.

'Well, nat'rally he'd disguise the smell,' said William.
'They're jolly clever at that sort of thing . . . Come on.
Let's go an' see what's in the other rooms.'

Walking on tiptoe, his face set and stern, he led the way
into a Victorian hall, with an old-fashioned hatstand and
an antlered head fixed on the wall. Silently, cautiously, he
opened the doors that led from it – a conventionally furnished drawing-room, a study with bookshelves round
the walls, a dining-room with heavy mahogany table and
chairs . . .

'He can't have stolen all those things,' whispered
Ginger. 'They don't look the sort of things people steal.'

Doubts were beginning to assail William, too, but he
quelled them.

'It's all part of his cunning,' he said. 'He's nat'rally got
it lookin' like a place a villain wouldn't live in jus' to put
people off the scent. I bet if we took up the floors we'd
find it full of stolen stuff. Or p'raps he's got it upstairs.
I'm goin' upstairs to have a look anyway.'

In silence except for the sound of their heavy breathing
the two crept up the staircase. At the top William hesitated
for a few moments then slowly opened the nearest door. A
bedroom with french windows standing open on to a balcony . . . William went up to the open window, stopped
short and gave a gasp of astonishment. For there, in a corner of the balcony, reclining on a deck-chair, reading a
book, was a tall, spindly, grey-haired man, dressed in a
scanty pair of bathing trunks, his bare feet resting on a
small woolly mat. He glanced up from his book. His eyes

THE MAN GLANCED UP FROM HIS BOOK AND HIS EYES MET
WILLIAM'S IN ANGRY AMAZEMENT.

met William's and seemed to start from his head in angry
amazement. His thin face flamed crimson and he leapt
from his seat with a bleat of rage.

Acting on the simple impulse of self-preservation and
completely forgetting his heroic role, William slammed
the french window and took to flight, scrambling down
the stairs with Ginger at his heels and out of the back door.

'Let's shut it quick!' he panted, drawing the door to
with a bang. 'Come on.'

They fled down to the gate. There William stopped. No
one was pursuing them. There was no sound, no movement from the house.

'Let's get away quick, William,' said Ginger.

Jumble supported his plea, leaping up and straining at his string in the direction of the road. William still stood gazing at the house.

'Can't make it out,' he said. 'Bet he *is* a fence, you know. If he hadn't got a guilty conscience, he'd have chased us. He's scared we've found out somethin'. He's prob'ly busy moving all his stolen stuff to diff'rent places. Taking up some diff'rent floors to hide it under 'case we've found out. I bet that's what we'd find him doin' if we went back.'

'Yes, but you're not goin' back, are you, William?' said Ginger anxiously.

'Not right into the house,' said William. 'He's probably put mantraps an' bombs all over it by now. I'm jus' goin' round to the back garden to have a look at that window. He was sittin' in a chair on a sort of ledge—'

'Balcony,' said Ginger.

'Well, whatever it is. He was sittin' there practically naked. I want to know what he was doin' there an' what he's doin' now.'

'Gosh, William!' said Ginger helplessly. 'We're lucky to've got out of the place alive an'—'

But William was already making his way round to the back of the house. Ginger followed with a mixture of excitement and apprehension at his heart. Jumble uttered an indignant howl, then laid his head between his paws with a deep sigh and abandoned himself to despair.

At the back of the house was a largish lawn surrounded by a hedge. After a moment's hesitation, William went boldly to the middle of the lawn and looked up at the house.

The man in the bathing trunks was still on the balcony.

He stood with his back to them twiddling with the handle of the closed french window.

Suddenly he wheeled round. His thin face was now a dull green. His gaunt body in the faded bathing trunks quivered with fury.

'You!' he sputtered. 'How dare you! How *dare* you! You shall pay dearly for this trick. I shall put the matter into the hands of the police.'

The airy fabric of William's imaginings collapsed. The indignation in the voice was a righteous indignation. Here was no criminal. Here was a law-abiding citizen, justly indignant at the outrage he had suffered.

'Imprisoned on my own balcony in this unspeakable state!' he continued.

'Yes, but look!' said William. 'Can't you jus' open the door an' go back into the bedroom an'—'

'Open the door?' repeated the man. 'You've slammed it to! You've fastened the burglar catch. It can only be opened from the inside.' His rage boiled over again. 'You little scoundrels! You young villains! How *dare* you! Waiting till you saw I was safely engaged in sun-bathing, then entering my house with burglarious intent and stealing whatever you could lay your hands on, no doubt. At your age! Juvenile delinquency at its most lamentable! Oh, we'll see what the police have to say about it. We'll see! We'll see!'

'Yes, but I didn't know,' expostulated William, slightly bewildered by the speed with which the tables had been turned. 'I can 'splain it all . . . Look! I'll go into the house an' open the burglar catch for you from the inside.'

'From the inside!' spluttered the man. 'You slammed the back door, too, didn't you?'

'Well, yes, but—'

'That's got a burglar catch on it too. It can only be opened from the inside once it's shut. And all my keys are in the pocket of my jacket in my bedroom. To think of all the trouble I've taken to outwit burglars only to be outwitted by a couple of ruffians, young in years but hardened in crime. To think that I just left the kitchen door ajar for the baker to slip in the loaf while I was sunbathing and – to be imprisoned here in this appalling condition without even a *pullover*.' He emitted a sound that began as a bellow of rage and ended in a moan of anguish. 'The sun's gone in and the wind's changed and I suffer from rheumatism in my shoulders.' He took up the mat from the floor of the balcony and slung it round his shoulders. 'I shall catch my death.'

'Hasn't anyone else got a key that'd fit?' asked William, remembering the occasion when the key to his mother's bureau had taken the place of the key to his father's suitcase.

'Yes, yes, yes, yes, *yes*,' spluttered the victim. 'My builder in Hadley has duplicates of all the keys, but' – bitterly – 'perhaps you'll tell me how I'm to get to him – marooned *naked* on this wretched balcony by a couple of young blackguards who ought to be in jail.'

'Well, listen,' said William. 'Ginger an' me'll go an' get them for you.' He turned to Ginger, who was watching the proceedings helplessly and in silence. 'Won't we, Ginger?'

'You will *not*,' said the prisoner, his anger rising again to boiling point. 'I wouldn't trust you with – with – with a tin-opener, much less a key. If I could get down I'd go to the nearest house with a telephone, ring up the builders and then hand you over to the police.'

William seldom looked beyond the immediate present. Retribution, he well knew, lay ahead of him, but for the moment his only concern was the rescue of the imprisoned sun-bather, and he was bringing all his ingenuity to bear on the problem.

'You could easily climb up on the roof from that balc'ny,' he said. 'Then you could sit on the roof an' wave your mat an' I bet someone'd see you an' bring a ladder.'

'Ridiculous! Preposterous!' said Mr Honiton.

'Well, you could climb down,' said William. 'You could stand on the top of that railing then get hold of the drain-pipe an' sort of let yourself down that way.'

Mr Honiton peered over the railing of the balcony at the drain-pipe that ran down beside it and drew back with a shudder.

'Preposterous! Ridiculous!' he said.

'It's easier than what it looks,' persisted William. 'I'll come up an' give you a hand.'

Without waiting for permission he set to work. He was an expert climber and drain-pipes presented little difficulty to him. Having come within reach of the railing, he put his hands on it to swing himself up. But William's form was solid and the railing was not. The railing was a fragile affair of wrought iron, worn away by rust. For just a second it bore the by no means inconsiderable burden of William's weight; then it collapsed with a noise that sounded like a sardonic chuckle, depositing William and itself on the ground beneath.

'Gosh, I'm sorry,' said William, extricating himself as best be could from the debris. 'I didn't mean to do that. There must have been somethin' wrong with it to start

MR HONITON TOOK THE PLUNGE
AND ENTRUSTED HIS THIN FORM
TO THE DRAIN-PIPE.

with. It'd prob'ly got eaten away by insects or gnawed away by rats or—'

He stopped. Mr Honiton was dancing with rage on the floor of his now dismantled balcony.

'Your father shall pay for this damage,' he said. 'Pay dearly. And so shall you. I might have been killed.'

'Well, I might, too,' said William.

'And serve you right if you had been,' said the captive bitterly. 'You'd have got no sympathy from me, my boy. Tell me your name and where you live and I'll get into touch with your father the moment I'm at liberty.'

William was wondering whether he could establish his position as the inhabitant of an inaccessible island to which he was due to return immediately when he saw Mr Honiton peering down at him intently.

'I recognise you now . . . Brown . . . I know your father. I know where you live. Oh, you shall be severely punished, my boy. I'll see to that.'

William's last frail hope of retiring anonymously from

the adventure died away. But retribution still lay in the future and his immediate concern was still the release of his prisoner.

'You could get down quite easy now that the railing isn't in your way,' he said. 'The drain-pipe's got sort of ledges where it's fixed to the wall. If you put your foot on that one an' held on to the drain-pipe an' then put your foot on the next . . .'

'I couldn't possibly. It's preposterous,' said Mr Honiton.

'But listen,' began William, then stopped.

With the courage of despair, Mr Honiton had taken the plunge. Giving a long shuddering sigh, he had entrusted his thin form to the drain-pipe and, clutching, slithering, scrambling, had arrived safely on the ground. He sat there for a few moments with his eyes shut, then rose unsteadily to his feet.

'I hope you will always remember,' he said, 'that you're responsible for the most agonising moment of my life.'

'Yes, I will,' said William, who felt that the memory might afford him some small comfort in the dark hours of whatever lay in store for him.

The woolly rug had fallen to the ground with its wearer and Mr Honiton picked it up and draped it again about his shoulders.

'You will accompany me,' he said loftily, 'to the nearest house with a telephone. There I will ring up the builder, then I will ring up your parents and inform them that I am putting the whole matter into the hands of the police.'

'But— *Gosh!*' said William. The release of his prisoner had been effected and now he could bring his attention to bear on the next step in the proceedings. 'It was a *mistake*. Listen! I can 'splain it all. Look! I'll mend that railing myself, I'll get a hammer an' some nails an'—'

But Mr Honiton, his rug draped about his shoulders was striding round the house to the front gate.

'Come along with me,' he said tersely. 'I know your name and address and if you try to escape it will be the worse for you.'

'All right,' said William resignedly.

As well as resignation there was in William's mind his usual reluctance to abandon an adventure before its final stage. When William had started an adventure he liked to be in at the finish.

They made their way down to the gate. Jumble's string hung Jumble-less from the gate-post. Jumble had evidently at last managed to detach himself from it and had streaked off for home.

'Thank Heaven I can take the path across the fields,' Mr Honiton was saying, 'so, if fortune is on my side, I shall attract little attention.'

The strange procession set out – Mr Honiton, his figure looking incredibly long and lank in his scanty bathing trunks and woolly mat, picking his way gingerly across the road, and William on one side and Ginger on the other.

But good fortune was not on his side. A small crowd of passing children attached itself to him, following him across the field, offering comments and suggestions.

'He's out of a circus. I *bet* he's out of a circus.'

'He's a Russian. I've seen pictures of 'em. They wear furs an' funny clothes . . .'

'He's an escaped lunatic an' he's bein' took back.'

At this moment Mr Honiton inadvertently placed his foot on a particularly virulent nettle. He gave a yell of pain and began to dance about, holding his foot in his hand.

'He *is* a lunatic,' cried the children in triumph. 'Look at him! he's *ravin'*!'

'I think he's a waxwork,' said a small boy. 'I think he's a waxwork an' they're tryin' him out. They've wound him up to act like that.'

''Course he's not a waxwork. He's yuman.'

'He isn't yuman.'

'He is.'

'He isn't.'

'All right. Go an' touch him an' see.'

'No.'

'I dare you.'

'No. He might be a savage.'

'I *dare* you.'

'A'right.'

Summoning all his courage, the boy who had offered the waxwork suggestion darted forward and plunged a small finger violently into the small of Mr Honiton's back.

Mr Honiton turned round with such a bellow of fury that the crowd stampeded back to the road as fast as it could.

'Outrageous! Preposterous! Disgraceful!' exploded Mr Honiton. 'How many more humiliations shall I have to suffer before I reach Miss Granter's?'

'Miss Granter's?' said William.

'Yes, yes, yes,' snapped Mr Honiton, limping painfully

MR HONITON GAVE SUCH A SHATTERING BLAST OF RAGE THAT THE
POLICEMAN MOUNTED HIS BICYCLE AND RODE OFF.

along. 'Haven't you enough sense to realise that Miss Granter's is the nearest house with a telephone? I barely know her. What she will think of me? The whole situation is mortifying in the extreme.'

'Gosh, Ginger!' said William, stopping short. 'The books!'

'What books?' said Ginger.

Events had crowded in on him so thick and fast that he had almost lost sight of their connecting link.

'The man's books, you chump!' said William impatiently. 'The books we meant to take back before five-forty-five for him to read in the train.' They were passing the open doorway of the old barn. He peeped inside. The books lay on the ground where he had left them. 'If we're goin' to Miss Granter's, I'd better take them.' He entered the barn and emerged with the books under his arm. 'Gosh! I hope it's not too late. He'll be mad if he's nothin' to read in the train.'

Mr Honiton, ignoring the interlude, strode on ahead, muttering fiercely to himself.

They climbed the stile into the further road. Miss Granter's house lay only a few yards away from them. But even so fortune was not on Mr Honiton's side.

A policeman was coming down the road on his bicycle. He dismounted and gazed in mingled amazement and perplexity at the trio that was approaching him.

'I'm sorry, sir,' he said, 'but we don't allow no nudist stuff around here.' Amazement and perplexity gave way to severity and disapproval as he added, 'And I'm surprised at a gentleman of your age going about the public road indecently dressed. I—'

Mr Honiton interrupted him with a blast of rage so shattering that the policeman mounted his bicycle again and pedalled off towards the police station to consult with Authority. This particular situation had never presented itself to him before in the whole course of his professional career and he thought he'd better make sure of his ground before he went any further.

Mr Honiton walked in at the gate of Miss Granter's house. William and Ginger followed more slowly. The door was opened by Miss Granter.

'Oh, Mr Honiton, come in,' she said. 'Do come in. Whatever's happened?'

Mr Honiton entered, pouring out the story of his tribulations.

'. . . locked out . . . locked out of my own house . . . sun-bathing . . . young blackguards . . . telephone . . . builders . . .'

So deep was his emotion that the story was completely incomprehensible and Miss Granter did not even attempt to comprehend it. She took down a man's overcoat from the hat-stand and held it out to him.

'Do put this on. It used to belong to my father and my sister likes to keep it hanging in the hall. She imagines that it might discourage burglars. Make them think there's a man in the house, you know.' She opened a chest and took out a pair of large leather slippers. 'We keep these, too. I sometimes find them a comfort in the evenings.'

'Thank you, *thank* you,' said Mr Honiton gratefully as he shrugged himself into the coat and put on the slippers.

Then Miss Erica appeared. She looked paler and more fragile than ever and there were red rims round her eyes.

'Here's my sister,' said Miss Granter. 'I've just had to break some rather bad news to her. I'm afraid we're both feeling a little upset . . .'

Miss Erica was peering short-sightedly at William and Ginger.

'They're the boys who were here before tea,' she said.

Miss Granter smiled at them.

'Yes, such kind boys. They helped us with the dusting . . . and now they've evidently been helping poor Mr Honiton in his unfortunate predicament.'

Again the fiery purple suffused Mr Honiton's cheeks and he struggled manfully for words to express his feelings. While he was still struggling, William put down the books on the chest.

'Are we too late?' he said. 'We meant to bring them back before but a lot of things happened. Has he gone? The book man, I mean.'

'Yes, dear,' said Miss Granter in a tone of mystification. 'He went some time ago.'

'Gosh, I'm sorry,' said William. 'You see—'

But Mr Honiton, who had not noticed the books while William was carrying them along the road, was staring at them, his eyes and mouth wide open. Enveloped in Miss Granter's father's coat, his feet thrust into Miss Granter's father's slippers, he now presented an almost human appearance. He seized one of the books and, going into the sitting-room, stood by the window turning over the pages.

'The seventeenth-century edition I've been searching for for years!' he said excitedly. 'I'm a Cervantes collector, you know, Miss Granter.'

'I didn't know,' she murmured.

'This has been the great gap in my collection. I've combed antiquarian book shops for it. I've advertised for it.'

'How odd!' said Miss Granter mildly. 'He just wanted them to read in the train.'

'Who did?' said Mr Honiton.

He had apparently forgotten William, Ginger, the builder and the police – everything except the books on which he was still gazing lovingly and reverently.

Miss Granter told the story of the man who had come to inspect her library. Mr Honiton gave an indignant snort.

'They were the only valuable books in the collection, of course, and he thought he could get them for nothing.

A cunning, contemptible trick. You're lucky and I'm lucky that it didn't succeed.'

'But I can't think how it didn't,' said Miss Granter with a puzzled frown. 'He put them in his case before tea and after tea he just took up his case and went . . . I can't think how they vanished from his case.'

William gulped and blinked and plunged into his story.

'Well, you see, we wanted to try out bein' this Don Quixote man an' havin' some adventures, facin' an' fightin' evil-doers an' suchlike, so we jus' sort of borrowed the books to find out about his adventures, an' we meant to bring them back before the man went to his train but we forgot an' left them in the old barn. We couldn't make out much about it 'cause the man that wrote them was so ign'rant. He didn't know any English so we thought we'd set out after the evil-doers on our own an' we heard Colonel Masters an' Mr Saunders sayin' that Mr Honiton was a crim'nal an' sold stolen stuff for thieves—'

'*What!*' said Mr Honiton in a voice that was almost a scream.

'Well, they said you were on a fence an' a public danger an' we knew a fence was a crim'nal—'

'So we went to your house to find the stolen stuff,' put in Ginger.

A gust of laughter swept over Mr Honiton.

'Of course, of course!' He turned to Miss Granter. 'They run the Conservative and Labour Associations respectively, you know, and they work in harness. They're fighting political apathy. They say that they don't mind which Association you belong to as long as you belong to one or the other. I'm a thorn in their flesh. I'm a first-class specimen of political apathy. I don't take the slightest interest in politics. I agree with whatever they say just to get rid of them.' He gave another cackle of laughter. 'It infuriates them and I'm afraid I take a malicious pleasure in it.'

'But they said "*fence*",' persisted William, 'an' this man in the story I read was a fence an'—'

'Yes, yes, my boy,' said Mr Honiton, 'but "on the fence" is quite a different expression. It means taking neither side.'

'Well, why didn't they *say* so, then?' said William. 'We've had a lot of trouble all for nothin'. An'—' the bleak prospect of retribution loomed nearer – 'we're goin' to have a lot more.'

Mr Honiton, holding two books in each hand, made an expansive gesture with both of them.

'Oh, we'll forget all that,' he said. 'We'll certainly forget all that. One might almost say I'm in your debt. My builder can easily fix up the railings again. Really, looking back on the episode, I find it most amusing.'

William stared at him in silent amazement.

'And now, Miss Granter,' went on Mr Honiton, 'I hope you will allow me to buy the books from you.'

'Of course,' said Miss Granter.

Miss Erica clasped her sister's hand.

'Oh, Lucy!' she said tremulously. 'Do you think—? Is it possible, after all? Torquay, I mean.'

Miss Granter patted her sister's hand reassuringly and smiled at Mr Honiton.

'You see, my sister's been ill and ought to have a holiday and we'd planned to pay for it by the proceeds of the sale so it was a great disappointment to her when—'

Again Mr Honiton's cackling laugh rang out.

'Oh, I'm not like your visitor of this afternoon,' he said. 'I shall pay the full value of the books. I shall give you the sum I offered when I advertised for them, and that, dear lady, will cover a good deal more than a holiday in Torquay.'

'Oh, *Lucy*!' said Miss Erica, starry-eyed.

William and Ginger walked slowly homewards.

'Well, I'm jolly glad *that's* over,' said Ginger fervently.

'I am, too,' said William. 'Gosh! He was bats, puttin' those burglar things on all his doors.'

'She was bats, too, lettin' that man take those books.'

'Yes, she was . . . So was the other one, makin' all that fuss about goin' to the seaside. I've been to the seaside. It's only sea.'

'We were bats, too,' said Ginger after a pause, 'tryin' to do that Don Quixote stuff.'

'Yes, we were,' agreed William. 'There was only one person that showed a bit of sense all through it.'

'Who was that?'

'Jumble,' said William.

Chapter 5

William and the Paying Guest

'You see, she's coming on Saturday, dear,' said Mrs Brown, 'and I keep putting off telling him. He does so hate having people staying in the house.'

William's brow wove itself into an intricate pattern as he pondered on the situation.

'Couldn't you sort of hide her up somewhere in secret without him knowing?' he suggested at last. 'Same as people did with exiles an' Cavaliers an' rebels an' Roundheads in hist'ry. He's out at work all day, so you could go about with her then an' keep her hidd'n up when he's at home.'

Oh, no, dear,' sighed Mrs Brown.

'But listen,' said William eagerly. 'It would be jolly excitin'. We could keep her hidd'n up in the loft. There's a camp bed there, an' it's jolly comfortable, an' she could lower a basket at the end of a rope through the trap door an' we could fill it with food an' she could draw it up again. I once read about someone doin' that an'—'

'No, William,' said Mrs Brown firmly. 'I must just go on hoping for the best. I've been waiting for him to be in a good mood to tell him but he's had this awful cold and it's been dreadful weather and he's been off his game at golf and there's something wrong with his tomatoes so that every evening he seems more in the dumps that he was before and – well, I keep putting it off.'

'Let her jus' come an' you pretend you didn't know she was comin',' suggested William. 'You can say, "Well, I'm jiggered! I thought you were in – Cyprus or somewhere." ' 'Oh, no, dear,' said Mrs Brown. 'Of course it's his never having met her that makes it more difficult. He hates strangers and he hates having people staying in the house, so – well, there it is!'

Mrs Brown had an aunt who had gone to live in Sydney before Mrs Brown met Mr Brown, had stayed there ever since, and was now paying a visit to England – her first for thirty years. Mrs Brown had invited her to spend a fortnight of it with the Browns. Aunt Susan had accepted the invitation and all that remained was to break the news to Mr Brown. And this Mrs Brown had been vainly trying to do for the last fortnight. At first she had put it off light-heartedly, confident that Fate would shortly give her some convenient opening. But Fate refused to co-operate. Each evening Mr Brown came home gloomy and depressed and so obviously in need of cheering up that Mrs Brown put off breaking the news of Aunt Susan's visit for yet another day.

It was unusual for Mrs Brown to confide her troubles to her younger son, but Robert and Ethel were away on holiday and, as Saturday crept nearer, she felt the need to confide in someone, however unsuitable.

'Tell her not to come,' said William suddenly. 'Ring her up an' say we've all got whooping cough.'

'No dear,' said Mrs Brown. 'I mustn't put her off, whatever happens. She saved my life once when I was about fourteen. We were at the seaside and I was swimming in the sea and she and my mother were having a picnic tea on the beach and I got into difficulties – I think I had a sort of cramp – and Aunt Susan saw what was happening. My mother was sitting with her back to me and anyway she couldn't swim, and Aunt Susan just flung off her coat without a second's hesitation and swam out and brought me back. So I couldn't bear to do anything unkind to her. That's why I'm anxious to catch your father in a good mood before I tell him, so that he'll – welcome her when she comes on Saturday.'

'Saturday!' said William. 'Gosh! It's only two days off.'

'I know dear,' said Mrs Brown with another sigh. 'I'm afraid I've let it slide rather a long time. I shall *have* to tell him this evening or tomorrow.'

'Well, listen! I've got an idea,' said William. 'Let me do something for him to put him into a good temper.'

'*No*, William!' said Mrs Brown. 'Anything but that!'

Mr Brown came home that evening looking tired and gloomy. He had been short-staffed at the office and had had to stay late. He had missed his usual train and the later train had been so crowded that he had had to stand for half the journey between a woman whose shopping basket dug into his stomach and a man whose umbrella point dug into his foot. He had waited ten minutes for a bus at the station and, when he finally set off to walk, the bus had passed him almost immediately afterwards, shooting the contents of a large puddle over his person as if in gleeful mockery.

A hasty inspection of his tomatoes increased his suspicion that they were suffering from yellow spot and a visit to his asparagus bed showed it clearly infested with rust.

His spirits rose slightly during the evening, but never to the point at which his wife felt if safe to mention the expected guest.

William did his best the next morning at breakfast.

'You're goin' to have a smashin' surprise tomorrow, Dad,' he said with devastating heartiness. 'Somethin' jolly exciting's goin' to happen to you.'

'Be *quiet*, William,' said his mother with a frown, and 'Don't talk with your mouth full,' said his father from behind his newspaper, and William reluctantly subsided.

'I'll tell him this evening,' said his mother when the two were alone again. 'Friday's generally a good evening. I'll lead up to it tactfully.

But this Friday wasn't a good evening. Mr Brown came home in a worse mood than ever. He announced as soon as he set foot in the house that he had 'another of his colds coming on'. He had a pain in his back and a pain in his chest and he'd sneezed three times in the train and twice in the bus and why was the hall carpet always crooked and if he'd told William once not to leave those wretched bows and arrows all over the place he'd told him a dozen times, and the front garden was a disgrace, nobody else's weeds seemed to grow at the rate his did . . . and Mrs Brown was kept so busy administering restoratives and soothing counsel that she had no opportunity to lead up to anything at all, tactfully or untactfully.

'It'll have to be tomorrow morning at breakfast,' she said to William. 'Well, it'll *have* to be, because she's coming in the afternoon. If he's got over his cold, he'll probably be in a good mood.'

By the next morning Mr Brown had got over his cold, but he was not in a good mood. It was unfortunate that the post had chosen that morning to deliver a formidable sheaf of bills. They included the gas bill, the electricity bill, bills from the builder, the ironmonger, the grocer, the chemist . . . His face darkened as he tore open the envelopes and inspected the contents of each.

'Well, I might as well go straight off to the workhouse,' he said.

'I don't think there are such things nowadays, dear,' said his wife. 'I think the Welfare State's done away with them.'

'I'm a ruined man,' said Mr Brown. 'Ruined! Here I am, working like a slave from morning to night, and all you can do is to fritter my money away on – on – on gas and electricity and – and' – he snatched up another bill at random – 'salt and soap powder and matches and kettles and—'

'Darling, I had to have another kettle,' said Mrs Brown. 'There was a hole in it.'

'—and dustpans and basic slag,' continued Mr Brown, ignoring her interruption.

'You asked me to get the basic slag for the garden,' said Mrs Brown. 'I don't even know what it is.'

Mr Brown had snatched up another bill.

'Why does that boy have to have a new pair of shoes every day of the year?' he roared.

'He doesn't dear,' said Mrs Brown, 'but sometimes things happen to them.'

'They sort of got caught up in a bonfire,' explained William apologetically.

Mr Brown was brandishing another bill.

'New glass in the greenhouse,' he roared. 'New glass in the greenhouse! Why doesn't he wreck the whole place while he's about it? Why does he stop at the greenhouse? Why does he leave a stone standing? Why doesn't he get some dynamite and blow the whole thing sky-high instead of doing it by bits and pieces like this?'

'I'm sorry,' said William.

He was going to explain the circumstances in which a sudden and inexplicable gust of wind must have deflected his cricket ball from its course and directed it on to the greenhouse when Mr Brown burst into another spate of eloquence.

'Well, we can't go on this way,' he said. 'Making straight for the bankruptcy court and the workhouse. We'll have to do something about it. We'll sell the house and live in a caravan. We – we'll emigrate. We – we'll take a P.G.'

Mrs Brown was not perturbed by this tirade. It took place with monotonous regularity whenever bills arrived in any appreciable quantity, and she knew that her husband would have forgotten the whole thing in an hour or so. What worried her a little was the fact that she had not yet broken the news of Aunt Susan's visit.

'Oh John . . .' she began, but her husband was already in the hall, collecting gloves, newspaper and attaché case.

'John!' she said again.

He was halfway down the garden path.

She took his hat from the rack and stood in the doorway.

'Here's your hat, dear,' she called. 'I think it's going to rain. You'll probably need it.' He came back for his hat, his face grimly set. 'Oh, and John, dear,' she said casually as she handed it to him, 'I may not be home by the time you come in. I'm going to meet Aunt Susan.'

Mr Brown stared at her.

'Aunt—?' he said blankly.

'Aunt Susan, dear. She's coming to stay with us.'

A dull red colour crept into Mr Brown's face.

'Coming—?' he said with ominous calm.

'Yes, dear,' said Mrs Brown. 'Coming to stay with us. She's the one who saved my life, you know. She's over in England and I thought it would be nice to have her to stay with us. I'd meant to tell you before but, what with one thing and another, I somehow didn't. Just for a couple of weeks, dear. I thought you'd enjoy it.'

'Enjoy it!' echoed Mr Brown, shifting his attaché case from his right hand to his left so that he could raise his right hand dramatically to the heavens. 'My privacy invaded! My home life shattered! My every meal poisoned by the presence of a chattering nitwit! Why not take a P.G. and be done with it? At least they pay for their keep. At least you can turn them out when you can't stand them any longer. At least they don't tell you revolting family anecdotes that you've heard a hundred times before. At least—'

'She won't do that, dear,' said Mrs Brown reassuringly. 'She's not a bit like that. You've never met her, so you don't know what she's like. And remember she saved my life.'

Mr Brown rammed his hat on his head in a gesture of uncontrollable emotion and stalked off to the gate.

Mrs Brown watched his figure till it was out of sight.

'Well, I've *told* him,' she said with a sigh of relief. 'He knows now.'

'What's a P.G.?' said William.

It so happened that in his short life he had not yet come across the expression.

'A guest – a visitor, you know – who pays money.'

'Gosh!' said William, surprised by the novelty of the idea. 'You mean that you jus' c'lect money from people that come to tea?'

'No, dear. You have someone staying in your house and they pay you money for staying in it.'

'It's a jolly good way of gettin' money,' said William. He considered. 'But I'd rather live in a caravan or emigrate.'

Mrs Brown laughed.

'Oh, your father didn't mean that, William. He was just getting things off his chest. He likes to get things off his chest, you know. Now run out to play, dear. I must make up Aunt Susan's bed.'

William went out and sauntered down the road. He met Frankie Parsons at the corner.

'I say, Frankie,' said William, anxious to air his new piece of knowledge. 'Do you know what a P.G. is?'

But you couldn't tell Frankie anything he didn't know.

'Course I do,' he said. 'They've got one at my cousin's an' ' – enviously – 'they have a jolly good time. She takes them to the pantomime an' the pictures an' buys them ice-creams an' lollies an' she's got a concertina an' she let's them play it.'

'*Gosh!*' said William.

Then Ginger hailed him by a raucous shout from the end of the road and he ran off to join him. After a spirited tussle for the possession of a stout hazel stick that their united efforts had dragged from the hedge, they went to

collect Henry and Douglas, and the four spent the afternoon trying to trace to its source the stream that flowed
through the wood, burrowing under bridges and through
ditches, varying the monotony of the search by paddling,
dam-building and water battles.

They continued the process in the afternoon, finding
themselves finally in Farmer Jenks's yard, from which
they were ejected by Farmer Jenks himself after the dog
that he had set on them (an old friend of the Outlaws) had
leapt up at them in rapturous welcome. At this point the
church clock struck five and the Outlaws decided that it
was tea-time.

'We've not really got to its source yet,' said Henry.

'We'll try again tomorrow,' said Douglas.

'We'll prob'ly find a spring gushing up out of the
earth,' said Henry.

'It might be boilin' hot like a geyser,' said Ginger.

'There might be gold in it,' said Douglas.

Cheered by these reflections, they separated to go home.

The day's activities had driven everything else out of
William's mind, but as he neared home the memory of the
scene at the breakfast table returned to it. Bankruptcy
court and the workhouse . . . They must be beastly places.
And he felt guilty on account of the shoes that had got
caught up in a bonfire and the greenhouse that, by some
inexplicable freak of nature, had received the full impact
of his cricket ball.

'Must have been a typhoon,' he muttered. 'That's what
it was, a typhoon. They slosh things round in circles an'
bang 'em about all over the place.'

But his spirit was weighed down by remorse. And
when William's spirit was weighed down by remorse it

knew no peace till it had made amends in some form or other. He regretted the impossibility of the caravan or emigration. He would have liked to live in a caravan or to have braved savage hordes of Red Indians in some remote foreign country. But there remained the P.G. William considered the prospect. A nice kind woman who would take him to the pantomime, buy him ice-creams and lollies, let him play her concertina and – most important of all – pay his father handsome sums of money for the privilege of living in his house. It seemed to solve the problem completely.

The bankruptcy court and the workhouse receded into the distance, but the problem was, how to set about getting a P.G. He might put a notice in the post office: 'Wanted a P.G. with konsertener and a lot of monny' – but people probably wouldn't see it till Monday morning and he wanted to get the thing fixed up as quickly as possible.

He wandered slowly and purposefully down the road. After all, he might just *meet* a P.G. There must be P.G.s about and there was no reason why people shouldn't meet them. But the village street seemed empty and deserted except for a few residents of long standing who, William felt, would view the prospect of even a short sojourn beneath his roof with acute disfavour.

Then, as he turned the bend in the road, his spirits rose. A woman whom he had never seen before stood by the roadside with a suitcase at her feet, looking round uncertainly. After a few moments' hesitation he approached her.

''Scuse me,' he said politely, 'but – er – but are you a P.G.?'

She looked at him suspiciously.

'Yes,' she said. 'Why do you ask?'

She was not a very reassuring sight. She was tall and thin with a small petulant mouth and small peering eyes. She wore an orange tweed suit that clashed with her brightly hennaed hair and a tweed hat set at an aggressive angle. She did not look the sort of P.G. who would take one to the pantomime or buy one ice-cream and lollies or even possess a concertina . . . but she was the only one available and William felt that he must make the best of her.

'Well,' he began and was just pondering how to explain the situation when the woman burst into an exasperated monologue.

' 'SCUSE ME,' SAID WILLIAM
POLITELY, 'BUT ARE YOU A
P.G.?'

'It's all *most* annoying,' she said. 'I've been staying as a P.G. with some wretched people in Berkshire, but it wasn't at all satisfactory so I decided to make a change, and a niece of mine has friends in this village who wanted a P.G. so she arranged for me to go to them. She called for me in her car this morning and we got on all right till we reached Hadley and then the car broke down. We took it to a garage, but it turned out that the repair would take a considerable time, so we decided to come on here by bus. Then, as soon as we were settled in the bus, Angela – my niece – discovered that she'd left her handbag in the car, so she went back for it. The conductor assured us that she had time to go to the garage and back before the bus started, but she *hadn't* come back by the time it started and it was then too late for me to get off, so I just came on alone. As I said, it's all most annoying. I was relying on her for everything. I don't even know the name of the house or the name of the people.' She wrinkled her brow.

'It was something like Smith.'

'Was it Brown?' said William.

'It might have been. Yes, I believe it was. Yes, I'm sure it was.'

'I'll take you there,' said William.

She picked up her suitcase.

'Well, I must say I don't want to stand about indefinitely like this. It's ridiculous. Do you know the people?'

'Yes,' said William.

'Is it far?'

'No.'

'That's a good thing. My nerves are literally shattered by this experience. My name's Miss Privet, by the way.'

They walked on in silence. Dark misgivings were forming at the back of William's mind. Perhaps he had acted a little precipitately. Perhaps he ought to have warned or consulted his family ... but he had been so carried away by the unexpected and providential appearance of a P.G. at the very moment when he had decided to look for one that every other consideration had vanished from his mind. He stopped at the gate.

'Here's the house,' he said.

Then suddenly his courage failed him. Hands thrust deep into his pockets, brows drawn together in a thoughtful frown, he sloped off down the road.

Miss Privet walked up to the front door and beat a sharp tattoo on the knocker.

Mr Brown opened the door.

'Mr Brown?' said Miss Privet.

'Yes,' said Mr Brown.

'You're expecting a guest?' said Miss Privet.

Mr Brown had spent the last hour trying to screw up his courage to face the arrival of his wife's aunt, trying to reconcile himself to the fact that for the next fortnight there would be no corner of his house that he would be able to call his own.

'Yes,' he said morosely, opening the door wider and standing back to admit her.

The woman was worse than his worst fears. He couldn't imagine how he was going to endure a whole fortnight of her. But she had saved his wife's life. He must never forget that.

'My niece will be following me shortly,' she said. 'She mislaid her handbag and had to go back for it.'

'She would!' said Mr Brown with a mirthless laugh.

Miss Privet threw him an icy glance, then looked disapprovingly about her.

'Rather a poky little hall,' she said.

Mr Brown gulped and swallowed but managed to remain silent. This woman, he reminded himself again, had saved his wife's life.

'Where's my bedroom?' said Miss Privet.

'I'll show you to it,' said Mr Brown.

He took up the suitcase and led the way to the room that Mrs Brown had so carefully prepared for her guest.

Miss Privet went to the bed and felt the mattress.

'Reasonably comfortable,' she said.

Again Mr Brown gulped and swallowed and again, by a supreme effort of will, managed to remain silent. He must never for a moment allow himself to forget that this outrageous female had saved his wife's life.

Miss Privet was lowering herself in an experimental fashion into the small easy chair by the window.

'I should like a footstool,' she said. 'A chair of this sort definitely needs a footstool.'

Mr Brown uttered a harsh indeterminate sound.

Miss Privet was now switching the bedside light on and off.

'Too strong,' she said. 'I like a twenty-five watt bulb for the bedside light.' She opened the cupboard that contained the overflow of Mrs Brown's wardrobe. 'I shall need all this space. Will you please have all these clothes removed?'

Mr Brown's face was purple with his efforts at self-control

Miss Privet threw another critical glance around her.

'There doesn't seem to be much room for my trunks,'

she said, 'but perhaps you have a box-room where they could be kept.'

'T – t – trunks?' gasped Mr Brown.

'Yes, they're being sent on tomorrow. Oh, and I'd like the bed turned round the other way. I don't like sleeping with my face to the light . . . After all, when one's staying at a place for several months, one wants to be comfortable.'

'M-m-months?' said Mr Brown in a rasping high-pitched voice.

He was telling himself yet again that this woman had saved his wife's life.

'Oh, yes, I hope to make my home here till after Christmas at any rate . . . Well, you may leave me to my unpacking. My niece should be here any moment now.'

Mr Brown stumbled blindly downstairs. He was in the throes of a nightmare. It couldn't be true . . . but it *was* true. For months to come the very air of his home would be poisoned by the presence of this outrageous female. He would have no peace, no comfort, no refuge . . . and he couldn't do anything about it because she had saved his wife's life.

He opened the front door and looked out. No sign of his wife. She had probably done a lot of shopping in Hadley and was now going the round of every shop in High Street in search of the missing handbag. She would want a cup of tea when she came in.

Grimly, doggedly, he filled the kettle and plumped it on the gas ring, then, feeling the need of some violent exercise as an outlet to his feelings, he went down the bottom of the garden and set to work digging with almost maniac fury in the potato patch.

* * *

William, accompanied by Ginger, was slowly wending his homeward way. He had described his discovery of the P.G. with an airy confidence that he was far from feeling.

'They'll be jolly grateful to me,' he had said. 'They needn't go to this bankruptcy court or this workhouse an' we'll all have a jolly good time.'

But the misgivings that had seized him when he saw his P.G. entering the gate of his home grew darker and stronger.

Suddenly they saw Caroline Jones approaching them. Her small round face wore a lugubrious expression.

'Hello,' she said.

'Hello,' said William. 'What's the matter?'

'We've lost our P.G.,' said Caroline mournfully.

'P.G.?' said William.

'Yes. She was coming this afternoon an' she's not come.'

'Oh,' said William thoughtfully.

'Aunty Angela – she's Mummy's friend that got her for us – came, but she'd lost the P.G. on the way, and we can't find her. We've looked everywhere. Aunty Angela's still out looking for her.'

'What's her name?' said William.

'Miss Privet,' said Caroline.

'Oh,' said William, more thoughtfully.

'She'd left the other place she was at because she didn't like it and Aunty Angela had fixed up for her to come to us.'

'Why didn't she like it?' said William, playing for time.

'Space men an' mice an' insects,' said Caroline.

'What?' said William, startled.

'She had an awful dream about a space man with a black face coming into her bedroom. She had it twice an' she thought it meant it was really going to happen an' it scared her stiff so's she felt she couldn't stay in the house another minute. An' she saw a mouse in her bedroom, too. A real one. An' that made her feel she couldn't stay in the house another minute. An' she left her newspaper on the verandah table one evening an' when she went to get it in the morning it was full of earwigs and that gave her another shock an' made her feel she couldn't stay in the house another minute, so Aunty Angela was going to bring her to us, but' – mournfully – 'she's lost her. An' now I won't have a bicycle for Christmas.'

'Gosh! Why not?' said William.

'Well when I asked Mummy for one for Christmas she said I could have one if we got a P.G. 'cause then she'd have enough money for it.' Tears invaded Caroline's voice. 'An' we got one, but we've lost her.'

The confused threads of William's emotions straightened themselves out. To have pinched the Joneses' P.G. was a trivial enough affair, but a bicycle was a serious matter.

'Well, listen, Caroline,' he said earnestly. 'Axshully I'm 'fraid I took her, but you can have her back. I'll get her back for you soon as I poss'bly can.'

'Oh, *thank* you, William,' said Caroline, beaming with delight.

She trotted on down the road.

'How'll you get her back, William?' said Ginger.

William's face wore the ferocious expression that betokened deep thought.

'I'll have to think out a plan,' he said.

Mrs Brown opened the front door and ushered her visitor into the hall.

'Well, here we are, Aunt Susan!' she said. 'I expect John's somewhere about . . . John!'

There was no reply.

'Perhaps he's in the garden. Or he may have gone out to golf.'

Aunt Susan – a plump pleasant-looking woman with white hair, kindly blue eyes and a humorous mouth – was throwing approving glances around her.

'What a charming house!' she said.

'Oh, it's quite small,' began Mrs Brown, then broke off with a cry of dismay.

'What's the matter?' said Aunt Susan.

'*Look!*' said Mrs Brown, pointing to the open kitchen door.

Aunt Susan looked. A kettle on the gas cooker was boiling over madly, pouring a torrent of water on to the floor. Already a large pool swamped linoleum and carpet.

'I'd better go and see to it,' said Mrs Brown, 'and then I'll take you up to your room.'

Aunt Susan laid a hand on her arm.

'Now don't bother about me, my dear. Just tell me where my room is and deal with the flood at your leisure.'

'Well, if you really don't mind . . . It's just to the right when you get to the top of the stairs . . . Perhaps I *had* better clear up this mess at once.

'Of course,' said Aunt Susan, taking up her suitcase and beginning to mount the stairs.

Mrs Brown hastened to the kitchen, burrowed under the sink for a floor-cloth and set to work on her mopping-up operations.

Aunt Susan reached the top of the staircase and opened the door of the room on the right.

A tall thin woman with a pursed mouth and red hair, wearing a suit of orange tweed, was standing in front of the dressing-table. She turned sharply as Aunt Susan entered.

'I don't know who you are, but will you kindly not come into my room without knocking,' she said severely.

Aunt Susan's placid mouth fell open in surprise.

'I'm s-sorry,' she stammered, hastily withdrawing and closing the door.

She wondered vaguely who the woman was. A sort of housekeeper, perhaps, or another guest. She hoped she wasn't another guest. She certainly wasn't going to be easy to get on with. She stood on the landing, looking about her uncertainly. Mary had *said* the door on the right, but perhaps she had meant on the left. Tentatively she opened the door on the left. It was Ethel's bedroom, but Mrs Brown had tidied and 'done' it since Ethel's departure, and it wore the air of a room prepared for a guest. Yes, this must be the room.

Aunt Susan entered and set down her suitcase. Inspection proved that drawers and wardrobe were full of clothes, but that didn't matter. Families always parked their surplus belongings in the spare room, and she could easily manage with her suitcase just for a fortnight. She went to the window. A pretty garden and a lovely view of the hills and woods beyond.

Mrs Brown mopped up the water, made the tea and went down to the bottom of the garden, where her husband was digging.

A WOMAN MR BROWN HAD NEVER SEEN BEFORE STOOD IN THE WINDOW.

'Oh, there you are, John!' she said. 'I thought you'd be here. Tea's ready.'

She spoke with perhaps rather over-acted brightness, tactfully refraining from mentioning the guest. Mr Brown raised his form to an upright position, leant his arms on his spade and looked at her.

'Mary,' he said earnestly. 'I shan't be able to stand it. I shan't be able to stand a single day of it. It's going to kill me. I only hope you won't regret it when it's too late.'

Mrs Brown laughed.

'Don't be silly, dear,' she said. 'I'll go up and tell her that tea's ready. You'll come in soon, won't you, dear?'

She retreated quickly into the house.

Mr Brown dug his spade into the ground with a ferocity that nearly threw him off his balance, then straightened himself again and let his gaze wander round him . . . It stopped short at the window of Ethel's bedroom. A woman he had never seen before appeared to be standing there, surveying the landscape. The light played strange tricks, he told himself. It must be the reflection of something or other in the window glass that just happened to look like a woman. More than once he'd thought the whole place was on fire because the windows caught the rays of the setting sun.

He dug hard for several minutes, then looked up again. The woman was still there. A plump woman with white hair and a blue jumper. Could it be hallucinations . . . or something wrong with his eyesight? It was some years since he'd had his eyes tested. He opened and shut his eyes several times, then looked up at the window again. The woman was still there. He laid down his spade and walked rather unsteadily towards the house.

Mrs Brown went upstairs, knocked at the door of the spare room and entered. Miss Privet stood by the bed, contemplating her suitcase. Her tight features were knit together in irritation and impatience. She couldn't think what had happened to Angela and she was certain she wasn't going to be happy here. (Five minutes anywhere was enough to convince Miss Privet that she wasn't going to be happy there.) She'd unpacked and repacked her suitcase and, if Angela didn't come soon, she was going back to those wretched people in Berkshire.

She turned an angry frown on to Mrs Brown.

'What do you want?' she snapped.

On a sudden impulse of panic Mrs Brown retreated from the room, closed the door and returned to the kitchen.

Mr Brown was just entering the kitchen from the garden.

'Mary—' he began.

'John—' began Mrs Brown.

Then, in the same moment, in the same breath, in the same words, they said:

'There's a strange woman in the house.'

'You've seen her, too?' said Mrs Brown, sitting down weakly on the nearest chair.

'Yes,' said Mr Brown. 'Have you?'

'Yes. A woman with red hair.'

'White hair,' said Mr Brown.

'In a yellow suit.'

'A blue jumper.'

'A thin woman.'

'A fat woman.'

Mr Brown, also feeling the need of some form of support, sat down weakly on the ironing stool.

'We've both gone mad, Mary,' he said solemnly. 'There's no other explanation.'

At this moment there came a loud knock on the front door.

Mr Brown gathered his scattered forces and went to answer it.

A girl in plaid trousers with her hair in a pony tail stood there. She looked brisk and efficient, but a little harassed.

'Is my aunt here?' she asked.

'I expect so,' said Mr Brown bitterly. 'We have quite a selection. Do you like them with red hair or white? Do you prefer them in blue jumpers or yellow suits? Do you like them fat or thin? Do—'

'John!' said Mrs Brown reproachfully, coming from the kitchen to join them.

And then Miss Privet appeared at the head of the stairs, carrying her suitcase. She put down the suitcase and descended.

'*There* you are, Angela!' she said reproachfully. 'Where on earth have you been?'

'Where on earth have *you* been, Aunt?' said Angela. 'I've been hunting for you for *hours*. I've been to almost every house in the place, and then someone said they'd seen you come here.'

'You told me that you'd arranged accommodation for me with some people called Brown,' said Miss Privet, 'so naturally I found them and came to them.'

'I said Jones, not Brown.'

'I'm quite sure you said Brown.'

'But what's *happened*?' demanded Mrs Brown hysterically.

A confused account of what happened followed.

'Oh, well,' said Angela at last,' you'd better come along to Mrs Jones as quickly as you can. The poor woman is distracted. We thought you must have met with an accident . . . I'm so sorry you've had all this unnecessary trouble, Mr Brown.'

Mr Brown's face wore a thoughtful far-away expression.

'Did you say it was a boy who directed you to this house?' he said slowly.

'Yes,' said Miss Privet.

'What sort of a boy?'

'Oh, just a boy,' said Miss Privet.

And then there came a sound like an earthquake. It seemed to shake the house to its foundations.

But it was only William, who had tripped over Miss Privet's suitcase and fallen headlong downstairs.

It was only William, his blackened face enclosed in his space helmet, his white rat Edgar in one pocket and a collection of earwigs (housed in a perforated matchbox) in the other.

It was only William carrying out his carefully prepared plan for the restoration of his borrowed P.G. to her rightful owners.

He had entered the house cautiously by way of the scullery roof and the bathroom window and he had been making his careful way to Miss Privet's bedroom to 'plant' the mouse (Edgar was the best substitute he could find) and earwigs and await his opportunity of appearing suddenly to her in the guise of the dreaded space man and so drive her back to the bosom of the Jones family where she belonged.

He landed in a crumpled heap in the hall, an eye and a knee heavily bruised by contact with the stairs, his space helmet twisted awry, his eyes gleaming horribly from his blackened face, Edgar trotting off over the hall carpet in one direction and a slow procession of earwigs in the other.

'What,' said Mr Brown sternly, 'is the meaning of this?'

William sat up and rubbed his bruised knee.

'Well,' he panted, 'I got her 'cause I thought you wanted one, but she's not ours really. She's Caroline's. So I said I'd give her back. That's all I've been tryin' to do. Give her back to Caroline where she belongs 'cause of this bicycle.'

Miss Privet had suddenly noticed Edgar and the procession of earwigs. She gave a scream and darted to the door.

'If I stayed in this house one moment longer,' she said, 'I should go mad.'

'And I,' murmured Mr Brown fervently 'should share your unhappy fate.'

He saw his guests off then returned to the hall, flung aside the space helmet and led his son to the kitchen.

'What's that revolting stuff on your face?' he said.

'Shoe polish,' said William. 'Black shoe polish. You see, she was scared of black space men, so I thought I'd try—'

'Be quiet! Clean it off and then come and give an account of yourself.'

WILLIAM LANDED IN A HEAP, HIS EYES GLEAMING HORRIBLY FROM
HIS BLACKENED FACE.

* * *

Mr and Mrs Brown and Aunt Susan were enjoying their after-dinner coffee in the sitting-room. An atmosphere of peace and serenity enveloped them. Mr Brown's face wore an expression of bland satisfaction. The nightmare was over. The outrageous female in the orange suit had gone, leaving in her place this placid pleasant little woman who had insisted on cooking the dinner (and had cooked a most admirable one), who said that she enjoyed working in the garden and hoped to clear it of weeds during her stay, who was knowledgeable about tomatoes and had assured him that they were not suffering from yellow spot and had even undertaken to spray the rust on his asparagus. So great was his relief that he was looking forward almost with pleasure to the two weeks of her visit.

'What a day!' said Mrs Brown. 'Would one ever have believed that even William could have made such a horrible mix-up!'

'Poor boy!' smiled Aunt Susan. 'He didn't mean any harm.'

'Harm!' said Mr Brown.

He tried to put a suitable amount of severity into his voice, but in his mood of relaxed contentment it was difficult to sound severe. He had felt that some condign punishment should be meted out to William, but had reflected that the bruised knee and eye were a fairly adequate retribution and had contented himself by dispatching him summarily to bed as soon as the last trace of shoe blacking had been removed from his countenance. As it was almost William's normal bedtime and as he was somewhat exhausted by the day's adventures, it was a punishment that left little ill-feeling on either side.

'It's certainly been a shattering experience,' continued Mr Brown, 'but—'

'It was terribly naughty of him,' said Mrs Brown, 'but—'

'I must say it was just a little bewildering at first,' said Aunt Susan, 'but——'

William was hanging out of his bedroom window talking to Ginger, who stood in the dusk below. Ginger had been unable to restrain his curiosity and had slipped round to William's to learn the latest developments of the situation.

'Oh, yes,' said William nonchalantly, 'she's gone all right.'

'Gosh!' said Ginger, impressed, 'so that plan of yours worked, did it?'

'Well, it did in a way,' said William, 'but—'

Chapter 6

William Gets His Fairing

The fair's coming to Mellings tomorrow,' announced William.

Mellings was a small village beyond Marleigh and each summer a fair, which was held in a meadow there, drew the junior inhabitants of the neighbourhood from miles around.

His family received the news without interest. Mr Brown continued to read the evening paper. Mrs Brown continued to knit a jumper. Robert continued to study a text-book with frowning concentration. Ethel was away from home, but her photograph, hanging on the wall above the radio, seemed to take on an expression of supercilious aloofness.

'I said the fair's coming to Mellings tomorrow,' repeated William with a mixture of pathos and defiance in his voice.

'We heard you,' said his father without raising his eyes from his paper.

William had just returned from an afternoon's activity with his friends. He sat slumped despondently in an armchair, his hands in his pockets, his gloomy gaze fixed on his muddy shoes.

'I'm goin' there with Ginger an' Henry an' Douglas,' he said, 'an' they'll all have money but me.'

The pathos of the situation seemed to him so heart-rending that, despite himself, a hopeful note crept into his voice. His family remained unmoved.

'There'll be merry-go-rounds and dodgems an' the Wall of Death an' a High Flyer an' a Moon Rocket an' a Wild Sea Waves an' I bet a whole lot of new ones since last time an' you can't go on any of them without money. You might jus' as well not go at all as go without money.'

His family made no response. He decided to intensify the note of pathos.

'It might be the last fair I ever get the chance of goin' to,' he said.

'Don't be ridiculous, William,' said Mrs Brown, stung into speech by this remark.

'Well, you never know what'll happen,' said William darkly. 'Lots of people in hist'ry died young. I've forgotten their names but I know they did. Well, the little princes in the Tower did, for two, anyway.'

'William,' said Mr Brown, looking over the edge of his paper,' 'you know quite well that I said you were to have no more pocket-money till the new glass in the garden frame was paid for.'

'I bet it wasn't me that broke it,' said William. 'The wireless was on playin' music an' I bet the music broke it. Someone once told me about a special note of music breakin' glass an' I bet the wireless was playin' jus' that special note jus' when my ball went on to that frame. Gosh! My ball went on it as gently as gently. It *couldn't* have broke it. It *must* have been the music.'

'You heard what I said, William,' said Mr Brown, turning over to the financial page.

'Well, there's fairings,' said William after a moment's

pause. 'Fairings are diff'rent from pocket-money. Henry's gardener says that when he was a little boy all his fam'ly used to give him fairings when the fair came. They gave him sixpence or a shilling or' – hopefully – 'half a crown to spend at the fair. Will you give me a fairing, Mother?'

'No, dear,' said Mrs Brown. 'As your father says, you must learn to take the consequences of your actions. You've often been told not to play with your cricket ball at the end of the garden.'

'Will you give me a fairing, Robert?' said William, turning his gloomy gaze on to his brother.

'Oh, be quiet!' said Robert impatiently. 'Can't you see I'm – studying?'

William sat up, forgetting his grievance for the moment in this new interest.

'What are you studying?' he said.

'Archaeology,' said Robert self-consciously.

'Arky – what?' said William.

'Oh, shut up,' said Robert.

'What exactly is it that you're going to do, Robert?' and 'A dig over at Mellings, isn't it?' said Mrs and Mr Brown simultaneously, turning their full attention to their elder son in order to dispel the slight feeling of remorse that their spasmodic efforts to discipline their younger son always caused them.

Robert laid down his text-book as if glad of a few moments' respite from it.

'Yes. You see, Mr Monson, the new man who's taken the Towers, is terribly keen on archaeology, and he found an old diary kept by the chap who had the place in the eighteenth century, and it said, "My son's tutor told me that he had seen some tiles of undoubted Roman origin on some newly ploughed land on my estate. This led to an interesting discussion on the passing away of the old empires." You see, archaeology didn't mean much in those days, but this chap's mad on it, and he got the idea that there must be a Roman villa somewhere on the estate and he's been turning the place upside down to find it.'

'Gosh! I wouldn't take all that trouble over any ole Romans,' said William, adding with disgust, 'They talked in Latin. They must have been dotty.'

'Shut up!' said Robert. 'Anyway, he's dug it nearly all over in bits and pieces and hasn't had a single find, so the whole thing may be a mare's nest.'

'A mare's nest'd be a jolly sight more int'restin' than those ole Romans,' said William.

'Shut up!' said Robert. 'They're doing the park now and they've almost finished it and still nothing's turned up. They're starting on the last lap tomorrow and they want volunteers, so I'm going along.'

'I hadn't realised that you were interested in archaeology,' said Mr Brown.

A faint colour invaded Robert's cheeks. He stammered slightly as he spoke.

'Well – er – I wasn't actually – I mean, I wasn't till – well, what I mean to say is that I only met her last week. Hermione, I mean. Hermione Monson. I met her at the Conservative dance in Hadley and she was telling me all about her father's dig at Mellings and – well, somehow we fixed up that I should go there and give a hand. She's wonderful, you know. Simply wonderful. You haven't seen her, have you?'

'No, dear,' said Mrs Brown, 'but I'm sure she's very nice.'

'Nice!' said Robert with a short sarcastic laugh. 'She's quite the most beautiful girl I've ever seen in my life. And she's intelligent and charming and cultured and – and – well, intelligent and charming and cultured. She's a wonderful actress, too. She was in the running for the cup at the Hadley Dramatic Festival, but the producer made hay of the show.'

'Sounds like a horse,' said William, 'out of this mare's nest you were talkin' about.'

'Shut up!' said Robert. 'Have you seen her, Dad?'

Mr Brown had taken refuge behind his evening paper again and made no answer.

'So you're going to start digging this hole in the park tomorrow, are you, dear?' said Mrs Brown.

'Yes, I start field work on the site tomorrow,' said Robert. 'It's the last hope. If nothing turns up they'll simply have to throw in their hand. But—' a tender, reminiscent smile curved his lips – 'Hermione said that perhaps I'd bring them luck.'

'Did you say it was at Mellings?' said William.

'Yes.'

'That's where the fair is.'

Robert threw him a dark and threatening glance.

'Don't you dare come near it,' he said. 'I'll skin you alive if your dare come near the place where we're digging.'

'Gosh! D'you think I want to?' said William contemptuously. 'These ole Romans can stay buried till the end of the world for all I care. Serves 'em right for talkin' in Latin.'

'It's a job, you know, that needs a certain amount of skill,' said Robert expansively. 'Method and – and, intuition as well as physical endurance and delicacy of touch in handling the finds. And, of course, one needs a knowledge of the historical background. Altogether it's quite an exacting science. I'm thinking of joining the Mellings Field Club and going in for it seriously. Hermione says—'

He looked round. No one was listening to him. His father was reading the evening paper. His mother was studying her knitting instructions. William had slipped from the room. He sighed and took up his text-book again. He read it with almost savage concentration, muttering such words as Verulamium, Opus Signinum, Camulodunum and Calleva Atrebatum.

William entered the kitchen where his mother was engaged in making a cake. He had watched Robert set off immediately after breakfast, dressed with elaborate carelessness in corduroy shorts, an open-necked sweater and a scarf of startling hue. Robert took a knapsack containing his text-book, a couple of trowels, a compass, several brushes, a tape measure (the text-book had recommended the use of a theodolite, but, as he had no idea what it was, he had omitted it) and a flamboyant box of chocolates that he intended to present to Hermione at some suitable stage of the proceedings.

'Wonder what he's doin', now,' said William, perching on the edge of the table and putting a handful of sultanas into his mouth. 'Gosh! He's dotty, isn't he? Diggin' up ole Romans! Gosh! Fancy wastin' his time diggin' up ole Romans! I'd sooner bury them than dig 'em up any day. *Mensa* an' *dominus* an' all that rubbish!' He stretched out his hand, helped himself to some more sultanas and continued indistinctly, 'If they wanted to talk, why couldn't they talk English, same as everyone else? I bet they'd nothin' to say worth listenin' to, anyway . . . They were all dotty, same as Robert an' that horse girl.'

'William, don't eat all those sultanas. I've just weighed them out for a cake.'

William surveyed the other ingredients with a critical frown.

'There's nothin' else to eat,' he said. 'I don't like candied peel.'

'You've only just had lunch.'

'Well, I get hungry jolly quickly after a meal. I'll wait till you've mixed it an' then I'll have a bit raw. I like it raw better than cooked.'

'No, William,' said Mrs Brown, remembering how many of her cake mixtures had vanished before William's onslaughts. 'You ought to be going out on a fine afternoon like this.'

'I am,' said William. 'I told you. I'm goin' to the fair at Mellings' – his grievances returned to him and he added – 'without any money.'

'Now, William, don't start on that again.'

William didn't start on it again. He had – a rare thing with him – expended all his eloquence on the subject. Moreover, he had reconciled himself to the situation. Ginger, Henry and Douglas would probably have money and the four always pooled their resources. There would be a certain humiliation in his position, of course, but the balance could be redressed at some future date.

'Well, run along, dear,' said Mrs Brown, delaying the process of starting the cake.

'Can I take some sultanas with me?' said William. 'I

don't want to go about on an empty stomach. It's jolly bad for people goin' about on empty stomachs.'

'All right,' said Mrs Brown. Though she was conscientiously supporting her husband's disciplinary action, she still felt a little guilty at the thought of William's going penniless to the fair. 'You can have some.' She took the jar of sultanas from the store cupboard and poured a generous dollop on to the table. 'That should keep you going,' she said with a smile. 'They're supposed to be nutritious. At least, it said so in an article I read about food values . . . Now don't put them loose in your pocket. Let's find a paper bag.'

William crammed another handful into his mouth, put the rest into the paper bag, thrust the paper bag into his pocket and set out.

He had arranged to meet the other three at the Mellings cross-roads. It happened that Mellings lay beyond his usual sphere of activities and this lent a certain novelty and excitement to the journey. The sun was shining and there was an exhilarating freshness in the air, and he enlivened his walk by various expeditions of discovery into ditches and the surrounding woodland, by vaulting over gates and climbing trees and doing a few ineffectual handsprings in the road. The handsprings landed him in the track of an oncoming motor cyclist. The cyclist, a youth of about eighteen, swerved, stopped, dismounted and gave him some terse home truths and a lesson in handsprings before he mounted his cycle again. Still further cheered and invigorated by this little encounter, William proceeded on his way.

It was when he was approaching Mellings that he came to the wall. Walls were always a challenge to William. He considered this one speculatively. It wasn't so low as to be unworthy of his efforts or so high as to be impossible. He peered over the top. The wall enclosed a rough patch of ground, a tumbledown cottage and, beyond the cottage, an orchard of ancient gnarled apple trees that merged into the surrounding woodland. No one seemed to be about. With a certain amount of difficulty, he hoisted himself up on to the wall and, holding out his arms to preserve his balance, began to walk along it. It was more difficult than it looked but he thought that he could just manage it. He got a little way beyond the middle, then, seeing the end within reach, quickened his pace . . . wobbled . . . clawed the air . . . and fell with a splash into the enclosure, for his cursory inspection had not warned him of a stream on the other side. He crawled out of the water, then heard a cackle of laughter and looked around. An old man was hobbling out of the cottage door.

'Thought you wouldn't do it,' he said gleefully. 'I was a-watchin' of you through the winder. You didn't do so bad, though. Got more 'n' halfway, didn't you? Didn't do so bad. But you lost your head near the end. Thought you would.' He gave another cackle of laughter. 'Not drowned, are you?'

'No,' said William, breathless from his fall and bewildered by his unexpected reception. He looked down at his damp, mud-stained person. 'I'm a bit wet.'

'You'll dry in the sun,' said the old man reassuringly. 'Come and sit in the sun and have a drink of ginger beer.'

'Gosh! Thanks!' said William.

'Come on,' said the old man.

William followed him to the cottage. A wooden table and a chair stood outside in the sunshine.

'Sit ye down,' said the old man.

He hobbled into the cottage and brought out another chair, returned to the cottage and brought out two mugs and a jug.

'You'll soon be dry,' he said again, as he poured the ginger beer into the mugs. 'Now try me ginger beer. 'Ome made, it is. You can't buy ginger beer like this in shops.' He raised his mug. 'Here's luck!'

William raised his mug.

'Here's luck!' he said.

It was delicious ginger beer, tangy and gingery. William's heart swelled with pride as he sat sipping it with slow enjoyment. Never before had anyone treated him in this adult fashion. It seemed the richest experience that life had yet offered him.

'Do you live here alone?' he said.

'Aye,' said the old man. His face was covered with wrinkles. He had watery blue eyes, straggling white whiskers and a long puckered, humorous mouth. He was gnarled and bent like his apple trees and a little tumble-down-looking like his cottage. 'Used to like it when I were younger but I'm gettin' past it now. Can't get about an' work the place same as I used to. Got rheumatics. Shockin' some days, they are. I'd like to go out to Canada an' join me daughter. She's out there an' she wants me to go.'

'Why don't you?' said William.

'Fare,' said the old man succinctly. 'She says she'd send it, but I won't be beholden. I've never been beholden in me life and I won't start bein' beholden now. Once I got out, there's plenty of odd jobs I could do to earn me keep. It's the fare. I won't be beholden.'

William sipped his ginger beer and considered the situation with a thoughtful frown.

'Couldn't you sell the place an' pay the fare with the money?' he asked.

The old man shrugged.

'No one'll buy it,' he said. He pointed to the plot of ground. Part of it was freshly dug, and a fork, stuck into the soil, marked the spot where the old man had stopped digging. Two sides of the plot adjoined the woodland. On the other sides were the wall and the cottage. 'Look at it. Them tree roots run right through it an' it don't get no sun.' He gave his cackle of laughter again. 'Bracken it grows an' tree seedlings but not much else. I used to manage to grow currants an' raspberries an' take 'em down to the shops, but what with rheumatics an' all I can't get 'em picked these days. An' then there's the birds from the woods. They've got to live, of course, same as the rest of us, but they makes free with everythin' I grows without so much as a by-your-leave. Seem to think I grows 'em for 'em special . . . An' the roof of me cottage lets the rain in, an' me apple trees don't 'ardly bear no more.' He grinned through his white whiskers. 'Not that I worries, mind you. I'm not the worryin' sort. Have some more beer?' He poured out the ginger beer and raised his mug again. 'Here's fun!'

'Here's fun!' said William.

'I likes a bit o' comp'ny now an' then, don't you?' said the old man.

'Yes,' said William.

He was enclosed in an aura of well-being and happiness. He felt that he would have liked this moment to last for ever – sitting at a table, drinking ginger beer and conversing with his new friend.

'Feelin' a bit drier?' said the old man.

'Yes, thanks,' said William. 'I'm practic'ly dry now.'

'Gingered up inside, too?'

'Yes, thanks,' said William.

'Good! An' where may you be off to this fine afternoon?'

'I'm goin' to the fair,' said William. His grievances returned to him. 'Without any money 'cause they wouldn't give me any.'

'Aye, that's the way of the world, that is,' said the old man. He rose slowly and painfully. 'Well, I'll be gettin' on with me diggin'. I'm goin' to try lettuces. Maybe the little devils of birds will leave 'em alone an' they'll allus take 'em in the shops.'

'Can I help you?' said William eagerly.

He longed to express his gratitude to his new friend in some practical form. Almost before the old man had answered he had reached the plot of ground, seized the fork, and was digging away energetically.

The old man fetched a spade and for some minutes the two dug in silence.

'There's a lot of stones,' said William at last.

'Aye,' agreed the old man. 'I takes 'em up sometimes an' puts 'em in that ole barrel.' He pointed to a barrel at the end of the plot. 'I'll be makin' a new path to the cottage one of these days when me rheumatics shift – the old one's sunk terrible an' trips one up if one doesn't watch out – an' the stones an' such-like'll come in handy for drainage.'

Again they worked in silence till William said, 'Gosh! Here's a penny.'

The old man looked at the coin without interest.

'A lot of 'em turns up,' he said, 'but they ain't no use. Foreign, that's what they are. Dropped by some foreigner

'HERE'S A FUNNY THING,' SAID WILLIAM.

some time or other, I reckon. I've tried 'em at the shop an' they won't take them. I puts 'em in the barrel with the other stuff. It'll all help with drainage for the path. Don't bother to put 'em in as they turns up. Slip 'em in your pocket an' empty them in the barrel when we've done diggin.'

Again they dug in silence till William said, 'Here's a funny thing.'

The old man threw it an uninterested glance.

'Jewl'ry,' he said. 'One or two of them's turned up. Sort of metal when you scrape the dirt off. Sort of brooch but they ain't no good. Broke. Pins gone an' such-like. It goes in the bucket same as the rest.'

William slipped it into his pocket and went on digging.

'Here's some pieces of pot,' he said.

'Yes. Bits of vases with bits of dec'ration on some of 'em if you scrape the dirt off. I reckon this 'ere place was once used as a fairground an' them bits o' jew'lry an' vases was prizes for houp-là an' coco-nut shies an' so on an' they left the broke ones lyin' about when they packed up. Untidy folk, them gipsies. Foreigners, most of 'em. I bet it was them dropped that foreign money about, too. Prob'ly got fightin' an' upset the till an' broke up the prizes an' got the police after 'em an' packed up.'

'It mus' be jolly exciting bein' a gipsy,' said William wistfully as he slipped the piece of pot into his pocket. 'I've often thought I'd like to be one. Sometimes I can't make up my mind between an engine-driver an' a diver, but gipsies must have a jolly good time goin' round to fairs an' things.'

'I'd stick to engine-drivin',' said the old man. 'You know where you are with an engine.'

They worked till they heard the church clock strike three.

'P'raps I'd better get goin', now,' said William.

'Right, nipper,' said the old man.

'Good-bye an' thanks for the ginger beer.'

'Good-bye an' call in again any time you likes.'

William strolled on down the road, past a group of cottages, past the church, the post office, then past two tall gates of wrought iron with brick piers and heraldic emblems, leading into a broad sweeping drive. A thick shrubbery bordering the drive gave way to open parkland, and at that point William stopped suddenly, his eyes wide with excitement. For there were several trenches dug in the park and several young people standing about or digging in the trenches. A bank of earth had been piled up at the end of the trenches. Small white pegs were stuck into the ground at intervals and spades and brooms lay about everywhere. His excitement increased as he recognised Robert.

Robert stood in a trench, wielding a pickaxe in a resolute if amateurish fashion. A girl whom William took to be Hermione stood near him, studying what seemed to be a plan. She wore jeans and a pony tail and had a long thin face. I knew she'd look like a horse, thought William with quiet satisfaction. His eyes took in further details. A man, wearing a panama hat, was wheeling a barrow full of soil to the bank of earth. There was a man behind the bank of earth, but William couldn't see what he was doing. A girl in a beach suit seemed to be working more intently than the others, but William couldn't see what she was doing, either. A man in purple trousers was bending over some absorbing task and a man with a handkerchief tied round his head was crawling along the ground in a slow mysterious fashion.

A large harassed-looking man with bushy eyebrows, wearing leather shorts that were obviously the trophy of a visit to Austria and a crumpled striped shirt, strode about among the workers, who besieged him with questions and appeals.

'Is this any good, Mr Monson?'

'What shall I do with this, Mr Monson?'

'Here's a funny-shaped stone, Mr Monson. Do you think it can *be* anything?'

An air of dejection lay over the party. It was clear that their efforts had so far been unavailing. But William's interest had been caught and held by the fascinating scene. He wanted to watch it at closer quarters. It would be quite simple, he decided, to slip into the shrubbery at the point where the wall that enclosed the house and grounds joined the hedge that enclosed the park. It was rather a thick-set hedge but he managed to squeeze through it. Fortunately the shrubbery was thick-set too, and he could crawl to the edge of it without being seen.

Crouching on all fours, he peered through a laurel bush. Yes, he could see much more from this point. The man in purple trousers was sifting soil through a sieve. The man with a handkerchief tied round his head was measuring the ground with a tape measure. The girl in the beach suit was making up her face and the man behind the bank of earth was eating a banana.

This should have satisfied William, but it didn't. He wanted to look into the trench that Robert was digging and see what was in it. (Robert had now laid aside his pickaxe and was taking a surreptitious snapshot of

Hermione. Hermione was pretending that she didn't know he was taking it.) He wanted to inspect the curious instrument, rather like a telescope, that was set up in the middle of the site. He wanted to look into the wooden hut that stood at the further end of the park.

The grass was fairly long and William, in his games of Red Indians, had accustomed himself to move through grass in a manner that, as he mistakenly imagined, gave no sign of his presence. He dropped on his stomach and began to wriggle his solid form through the grass.

'I'm afraid we shall have to face defeat,' he heard Mr Monson saying gloomily.

'But, Mr Monson,' said the girl in the beach suit, 'I've got a *wonderful* idea for a poem about it. I know it's not as good as actually *finding* something, but I feel it's better than nothing.'

Then suddenly they saw William.

Mr Monson dived down and grabbed him by the neck.

'What are you doing here, you little ruffian?' he roared, jerking him to his feet.

William was not a reassuring spectacle. He had fallen into a stream. He had dug the old man's plot, carrying away generous portions of it on shoes, face and hands. He had scrambled through a hedge. He had crawled through grass.

'What do you *mean* by it?' continued Mr Monson, raising his voice to a bellow.

William tried to wriggle out of his grasp and, in so doing, kicked over one of the small white pegs. A howl of indignation arose. The nerves of the party were frayed by the failure of their 'dig', and they were glad to find an outlet for their exasperation.

'Look at him! Kicking over the surveying pegs!'

'The cheek!'

'The little wretch!'

Through the crowd William could see Robert's face, crimson with mortification.

'Who on earth *is* he?' shrilled Hermione. 'He looks simply *frightful*.'

'How *dare* you come trespassing on my property?' said Mr Monson. 'I've a good mind to hand you over to the police.'

Still wriggling in Mr Monson's iron grasp, William tried desperately to think of some excuse for his presence . . . and suddenly remembered the sultanas.

'I came to see Robert,' he said. 'I've come on a special message to Robert. It's somethin' very important.'

He shook of the restraining hand and approached Robert, whose face was a mask of horror, fury and despair.

'Go away!' said Robert hoarsely. 'Go away!'

'But who *is* he?' said Hermione. 'I've never seen any-one so frightful in my life.'

'They're to keep you goin',' said William, plunging his hand into his pocket. 'They're nourishin'. They've got food values. They'll give you strength for all this diggin' you've got to do.' He found that he had forgotten to empty his pocket of the oddments he had picked up on the old man's plot. He threw them carelessly on to the ground and brought out a sodden bag of sultanas.

A strangled growl issued from Robert's lips but it was drowned by a shout from Mr Monson. He picked up the piece of metal, rubbed off the dirt and examined it closely, his face working with some violent emotion as he did so.

'It's only an ole piece of jew'l'ry,' said William. 'A brooch or somethin' left behind by gipsies. It isn't any good. It's broke.'

'Heavens above!' said Mr Monson faintly. 'It's a dragon fibula. Second century, I should think.'

The man in the panama hat had picked up the piece of pottery and was scraping it clean, his eyes growing wider and wider.

'Prizes for houp-là an' things at some sort of fair,' said William in further explanation. 'Broke to smithereens. No good, any of 'em.'

The man in the panama hat seemed to find his voice with difficulty.

'Samian ware, by all that's wonderful,' he said.

A young man in a sleeveless jumper and an eyeshade, carrying a two-foot rule, had picked up the coin.

'It's foreign,' William warned him. 'It's no good tryin' to buy somethin' with it. The shop won't take it.'

'But this is incredible, incredible,' said Mr Monson in a quavering voice.

'There's lots more in an ole barrel where these came from,' said William, 'but you can't have 'em 'cause he wants them for drainage for his path.' He looked at Robert. Robert was opening and shutting his mouth as if gasping for air. He was obviously in no state to appreciate sultanas. William handed the bag with a courteous gesture to Mr Monson. 'Have a sultana . They got a bit wet when I fell into a stream but I 'spect they taste all right.'

Mr Monson waved the bag aside. William took out a handful and put them into his own mouth.

'It's fantastic,' said Hermione. 'It's too fantastic for words. He's the most frightful-looking boy I've ever seen

A STRANGLED GROWL ISSUED FROM ROBERT'S LIPS AS WILLIAM
THREW THE FRAGMENTS ON THE GROUND.

in my life and he springs up from nowhere with his
pockets full of the most fantastic finds and he just stands
there chewing currants.'

'I shall have to alter the poem if this leads to anything,'
said the girl in the beach suit thoughtfully. 'I shall have to
take out the note of frustration. A pity, in a way, because

it was such a good modern note, but it can't be helped.'

'Where did you find these things?' said Mr Monson.

'Jus' down the road,' said William. 'I'll take you there, if you like.'

They set out down the road. William walked first, occasionally plunging his hand into his pocket and

cramming a few more sultanas into his mouth. Mr Monson walked behind him. His face wore a purposeful expression, but every now and then he blinked violently as if to assure himself that he was awake.

Next came Robert and Hermione.

'Isn't it fantastic!' said Hermione in her thin high-pitched voice.

Robert said nothing. He was still beyond speech. Events had moved too fast for him.

The old man was still digging in his plot when they reached the cottage.

'Can they have a look at those broke things in your barrel?' said William.

The members of the Field club emptied the barrel and fell upon its contents like vultures on their prey.

'Tesserae!'

'Here's a bit of Castor ware . . .'

'This is part of a tile!'

'But who *is* the frightful boy?' said Hermione again.

The power of speech returned to Robert.

'He's my brother,' he admitted abjectly.

'Oh, Robert, darling, then you *have* brought us luck. I knew you would!'

Mr Monson straightened himself and looked round the plot, cottage and orchard.

'I should say the villa's just here,' he said. 'It was probably part of the estate when the diary was written.'

The old man approached them with his crab-like rheumatic gait.

'When you've quite finished makin' free with my property . . .' he said grimly.

'Now, listen, my good man,' said Mr Monson. 'We

have reason to suppose that there are the remains of a Roman villa beneath this site and we want to excavate.'

'Well, if you wants it you can buy it, can't you?' said the old man.

'I should be only too pleased to do so,' said Mr Monson.

'At my price,' stipulated the old man.

'Certainly, certainly,' said Mr Monson.

'Enough to get me to Canada with a bit over?'

'Of course.'

The old man's eyes went round the gathering to rest on William, who stood on the outskirts, munching sultanas.

'An' a fairing for the nipper, he said.

'Fairing?' repeated Mr Monson in a puzzled voice.

'He wants to go to the fair,' explained Robert, 'but he hasn't any money.'

They crowded round William. They had not much money with them, but what they had they showered on him – half-crowns, – two-shilling pieces, sixpences, a ten-shilling note.

'Gosh! *Thanks!*' said William.

Then he turned to the gate. He had, he felt, extracted from the situation all the savour it was capable of yielding. The thought of Mellings fair now filled his horizon. He hurried down the road to the cross-roads, where Ginger, Henry and Douglas were waiting for him.

'Thought you were never coming,' said Henry as the four set off up the short hill that led to the fair-ground.

'An' we've not got much money,' said Douglas gloomily. 'We've only got elevenpence halfpenny between us. How much have you got?'

'Pockets full,' said William airly. 'More 'n you could count.'

'Gosh!' said Ginger with a gasp. 'How did you get it?'

William was already reconstructing his recent adventure in his mind.

'Well, they jus' didn't seem to know how to set about findin' old Roman remains,' he said, 'so I had to show 'em an' they were so grateful that—'

They had breasted the brow of the hill. Below them stretched the fair-ground – gay tents, streaming banners, caravans, shooting galleries, dodgems, the High Flyer . . . The lilting strains of the merry-go-round filled the air.

William took out his ten-shilling note and waved it exultantly.

'Come on!' he shouted.

They ran down the hill to the fair-ground.

Chapter 7

William and the Television Invention

'When I think of them doin' *'er* an' not me, it makes me blood boil,' said Mrs Bott.

'Have another sandwich,' said Mrs Brown soothingly.

Mrs Bott took another sandwich.

'I've got half a dozen pergolas in the rose garden an' she ain't got one,' said Mrs Bott, slicing her sandwich with an air of ferocity. 'An' as fer garden ornaments, I've got gnomes an' storks an' such-like all over the place an' all she's got is some mouldy ole second-'and stone statue that came from It'ly or some such outlandish place.'

'Don't think of it,' said Mrs Brown.

'I can't 'elp thinkin' about it. *H*elp,' said Mrs Bott. (Occasionally Mrs Bott picked up her aitches as they fell and occasionally she let them lie.) 'I've got me proper pride, 'aven't I, same as everyone else. An' they showed 'er c'lection of silver. Well, what about *my* c'lection of silver? Brand noo, mine is, an' hers is mouldy ole stuff 'er great-grandfather or such-like 'ad to start with. Why, Botty paid *hundreds* of pounds fer our silver. An' 'er jew'l'ry's mouldy ole stuff, too. Botty paid thousands and *thousands* for me jew'l'ry. Diamonds an' such-like. An' they do *'er* an' not me!'

The television had recently been running a series of interviews called 'Gracious Homes and Hostesses', which Mrs Bott had watched with dispassionate awe and interest till her neighbour, Lady Torrance of Steedham Grange, had appeared in it. Then her proper pride had asserted itself and her sense of grievance had risen to fever pitch. Mrs Bott's sense of grievance was always ready to rise to fever pitch at the least excuse. And just at present she was ripe for an attack. Her husband was away on a business trip and her daughter, Violet Elizabeth, was away at school and, without a sense of grievance, she would have been feeling bored. She had come to tea to Mrs Brown's, prepared to pour out the whole story, and she was pouring it out in a torrent that swept everything before it.

'Forget it,' said Mrs Brown.

Mrs Bott didn't want to forget it.

'An' they 'ad 'er – *her* – sittin' in 'er drawing-room with a lot of old-fashioned stuff clutterin' up the place. Brand noo, all our stuff is. Why, the curtings alone cost 'undreds of pounds – *h*undreds. An' I bet I'm more of a *hostess* than what she is any day of the week. I 'ad – *h*ad – the Women's Institute to tea last summer – the whole boilin' of 'em – *an*' the Sunday School Treat, but never again! Why, I've 'ad a J.P. an' an M.P. *an*' a church-warden to tea, all in the same week, an' – an' they've got the nerve to do 'er an' not me.'

'Write to them,' said William.

Mrs Bott, who had forgotten that William was there, turned to look at him.

William sat on a low chair by the tea table, helping

himself to such cakes and biscuits as his mother had not thoughtfully put beyond his reach. His face was frowning and earnest, though his jaws kept up a brisk rhythmic movement as a pile of rock cakes on a plate near him rapidly diminished. It happened that William, too, was feeling bored. It was the summer holidays. Ginger, Henry and Douglas were all at the seaside, and the Browns were not taking their holiday till the end of the month. Normally William would not be having tea in his mother's sitting-room. Normally he would have no thought or interest to spare for Mrs Bott's troubles. But time was lying heavy on his hands and he was ready to take an interest in anyone or anything.

'Write to them,' he said again, fixing his earnest scowling gaze on the visitor.

'I 'ave done. *H*ave,' said Mrs Bott. 'An' they didn't even answer. I told 'em all about this money Botty's made out of 'is sauce an' about me silver an' me jew'l'ry *an*' about the car an' all. Brand noo, this year's model, our car is. Biggest car on the road. An' them there Torrances' car is three years old, if it's a day. 'Arf the size of ours, it is, too. You could get the whole thing into our boot. An' they've got the nerve to do '*er* an' not me.'

'P'r'aps Commercial'd do it if you let them advertise the sauce,' suggested William, still intent on helping her solve her problem.

Mrs Bott fixed him with an ominous glare.

'*What* d'you say?' she said.

'That's enough, William,' said Mrs Brown nervously. It was obvious that only a spark was needed to cause a grand explosion of Mrs Bott's wrath and equally obvious that William, if not speedily removed, would supply the spark. Already Mrs Bott's nostrils were quivering, her colour rising. 'Go out and play, dear.'

William, swallowing the last remnants of the rock cake, went out and played. He found Victor Jameson, also at a loose end, and the two spent the hours before bedtime very pleasantly, trying (without success) to make a 'suspension bridge' over the stream in the wood with the aid of William's mother's clothes-line and Victor's brother's cricket stumps.

William returned home at bedtime, damp and exhilarated, and gave no further thought to Mrs Bott and her problems till the next morning, when he came on her plodding along the road to the bus stop, her small plump face set in lines of anger and dejection.

'G'morning,' William greeted her.

She glared at him and proceeded on her way without speaking. William's interest in the situation revived. Mrs Bott, as a pedestrian, was an unusual sight in the neighbourhood. She was wont to travel even the shortest distance in a luxurious limousine behind a uniformed chauffeur. It seemed to be all that her small fat feet, on incongruously high heels, could do to carry her slowly and laboriously along the road.

William joined her and began to walk by her side.

'It's a nice day, isn't it?' he said pleasantly.

He had noticed that among grown-ups a discussion of the weather was a necessary preliminary to any conversation.

She made no response.

'Nicer than it was yesterday,' said William.

She plodded on in silence.

'I bet it's goin' to be nice tomorrow,' said William. 'It was jolly nice all last week, wasn't it? I forget what it was like the week before, but I bet it was all right then, too.'

Mrs Bott gave a snort that discouraged further pleasantries.

'I bet it's goin' to be all right next week, too,' said William, undaunted, then, considering that the weather had been adequately dealt with, turned on her the glassy smile that was wont to accompany his efforts at social intercourse with the adult world and plunged abruptly into the heart of the mystery. 'Where are you going?'

Mrs Bott gave another snort and suddenly took up the tale of her grievances again. William was an unsatisfactory audience but he was better than none.

'They've walked out on me,' she said stormily.

'Who?' said William.

'Me Staff. Chauffeur an' all. I told 'em what I thought of 'em this mornin'. Told 'em they was a pack of good-fer-nothin's. Well' – she paused for a moment to consider – 'maybe I said a bit more than that, but' – a note of pathos crept into her voice – 'I've been that worried over this telly business that there's times I 'ardly know what I'm sayin' an' what I'm not. *H*ardly. Anyway, they jus' packed up an' went. Said some things to me I wouldn't soil me lips repeatin' an' packed up an' went. An' me with all this telly worry preyin' on me mind! Would you believe it?'

'Yes,' said William absently.

Mrs Bott's troubles with her staff were a never-ending source of interest in the neighbourhood.

Mrs Bott threw him a suspicious glance.

'What d'you mean, yes?' she snapped.

'No,' said William.

She grunted.

'An' 'ere's me,' she said, 'with a car that'd take me a dozen times over, got to walk to the bus stop to go into

'Adley to get a noo staff of good-fer-nothin's. *Walk*, mind you, with a car in the garage that cost Botty five thousand quid if it cost 'im a penny!' She stopped and continued mournfully, 'I don't think me feet'll stand much more of it. I'd try this 'ere 'itch-'ikin' if I knew 'ow you did it.' She flung out an arm and pointed a finger at a passing lorry then stood scowling after it as it vanished from sight. 'There, you see! I might be a graven image for the notice they take of me. Serve 'em right if I dropped down dead.'

'I bet I can stop one for you,' said William. 'Let's wait for the next.'

They stood together in the road till a small sports car turned the corner and approached them. As it approached, William cocked his thumb in an elaborate 'hitch-hike' gesture. The driver looked at the ill-assorted couple – the small tousled boy and the stout woman in mink coat and feathered hat – grinned derisively and went his way. The driver of the next car, a shining elongated Jaguar, did not even look at them, though William added a raucous shout to his hitch-hike gesture.

'Saucy 'ounds!' said Mrs Bott. Then she turned the full force of her ill-humour on to her companion. '*You're* not much good, are you? Thought you said you could stop 'em. Good-fer-nothin', same as all the rest, that's what you are, William Brown.'

William had prided himself on his hitch-hike gesture and was feeling humiliated by its failure. A look of determination came over his grubby countenance.

'I bet I stop the next one,' he said.

And he stopped the next one. He stopped it by the simple process of stepping into the middle of the road so that the driver must pull up or run him down. The driver

pulled up. He was a good-looking young man with blue
eyes and crisply waved golden hair. William awaited the
full blast of his displeasure, but it did not come. The
young man, indeed, hardly looked at him. He fixed his
eyes on Mrs Bott, noting the mink coat, the pearls that
encircled her short stout neck and the diamonds that glit-
tered on her fat little fingers.

'Can I help you, madam?' he said deferentially.

Mrs Bott was radiant with relief.

'Oh, that's *hever* so kind of you,' she said. 'I reelly
don't know what I was goin' to do. Droppin' clean off
me, me feet were.'

'It would be a pleasure to give you a lift,' said the
young man. 'Where are you going?'

'I dunno if 'adley's out of your way,' said Mrs Bott.
'*H*adley.'

'Your way is my way,' said the young man gallantly.
'Hadley it shall be.'

He leapt from the driving seat, opened the door of the
front passenger seat and ushered Mrs Bott in with a courtly
bow. It was a smaller car than Mrs Bott was used to, but
she managed to squeeze herself into it and settled down
with a grunt. Neither of them took any notice of William. It
was clear that both considered his part in the proceedings
to be over. But William never liked to leave any adventure,
however casual, half finished, so he opened the back door
and climbed into the back seat just as the car was starting.

Mrs Bott launched once more into the story of her
grievances. It was by this time so confused that one would
have thought it impossible to disentangle it, but the young
man seemed to understand. He made suitable exclamations
of sympathy and indignation at all the correct points.

'I bet I've got twice as much silver than what she's got, fam'ly or no fam'ly. Solid. Brand noo. None of your old junk. An' just fancy 'em doin' '*er* an' not me!'

'Preposterous!' said the young man.

'An' the whole lot of 'em walkin' out jus' 'cause I told 'em what I thought of 'em – an' not a word that wasn't true a dozen times over.'

'Outrageous!' said the young man.

'I'd have told them a bit more if I'd known what they was goin' to do.'

'Perhaps you're as well off without them.'

'I dunno about that. Me with that great empty 'ouse – *house* – commodious mansion, they called it in the advert when Botty an' me bought it – an' no one as much as to make me a cup o' tea!'

'Botty?' queried the young man.

'Me hubby, Botty is. 'E's away on business an' won't be back till next week. He'd go ravin' mad if he knew all this trouble I'm in. He knows I'm 'ighly strung an' can't stand upsets. They go straight to me nerves, do upsets.'

'How dreadful for you!' said the young man. His voice was tremulous with sympathy.

'An' me jew'l'ry!' said Mrs Bott, returning with bewildering rapidity to her other grievance. 'I bet that Lady Torrance 'asn't got nothin' to touch it. Why, I've got more di'monds than I can wear at the same time, 'cause I've tried. *An*' a sapphire necklace an' an em'rald bracelet. They're all in a safe be'ind a picture in me bedroom. I bet they're worth twenty thousand if they're worth a penny. I'll say that for Botty. 'E don't buy rubbish. If 'e can't pay a good stiff price for a thing 'e won't buy it at all. Jacobean chairs she's supposed to 'ave an' I've seen 'em.

Velvet seats that worn I wouldn't be seen dead on. An' jus' think of 'em doin' '*er* and not me!'

'Extraordinary!' said the young man. They had reached the outskirts of Hadley and he slowed down the car. 'What part of Hadley do you want to go to?'

'Servants' Agency,' said Mrs Bott morosely. 'I've got to replace them good-fer-nothin's, though I don't for a minute expect I'll find anything better. *Would* you believe it – they'd got the sauce to tell me, last time I went there, that I'd got a bad name as an employer. *Me!* I couldn't believe me ears.'

'Fantastic!' said the young man. He had stopped the car in a small road that led into the High Street. 'I think the whole thing is so outrageous that I'd like to help you, if I can.'

Mrs Bott was touched.

'That's hever so kind of you,' she said, 'but I don't see 'ow you can. *H*ow. It isn't as if you was someone on television.

The young man smiled.

'But that's the odd part of the whole thing. You see, I *am* someone on television.'

Mrs Bott gaped at him.

'Go on!' she said incredulously.

'It's quite true,' said the young man, 'and I think I could fix up an interview with you for this "Gracious Hostess" programme.'

'Crikey!' said Mrs Bott weakly.

'I can't think why you weren't included in the first instance. It must have been an oversight.'

'I wrote to 'em,' said Mrs Bott. 'They never as much as answered.'

'Letters get lost in the post,' said the young man. He

was frowning thoughtfully. 'Actually I think I could manage to fix it up for this afternoon.'

'I dunno as I could manage it for this afternoon,' said Mrs Bott doubtfully. 'I'd 'ave to 'ave a bit of time to get things ready.'

'A pity!' said the young man, 'because this afternoon is the only time I could arrange it. We television blokes, you know' – he gave a short laugh – 'get booked up with work for months ahead. It's just an odd coincidence that I happen to have this afternoon free.'

Mrs Bott set her mouth grimly.

'Well, then, there ain't no time to lose,' she said. 'I'd better get busy gettin' this 'ere staff. I'll 'ave me work cut out to get 'em all settled in by this afternoon.'

The young man laid his hand on her arm.

'No, that's just what I *don't* want you to do,' he said.

She stared at him in bewilderment.

'What d'you mean?' she said. 'I've got to 'ave a staff, 'aven't I, for a telly show. What'd they think of me in a gracious 'ome – *h*ome – without no butler nor nothin'? Why, the money Botty pays out in wages 'd make your 'air stand clean on end, it would. Well, how're they to know that if they don't see a staff? Why, they'd all laugh their 'eads off at me. *H*eads.'

'Now listen,' said the young man persuasively. 'I want your programme to be something *different*. All these "Gracious Homes" shows have been more or less the same. Views of beautiful homes and beautiful hostesses, with servants in the background. I want yours to be *different*. You have a beautiful home and you are a beautiful hostess' – Mrs Bott smirked and bridled – 'but people are tired of that sort of thing. They want something different, something more up-to-date. They don't want to see the hostess just sitting about looking beautiful.'

'I look a treat in me noo blue silk,' said Mrs Bott wistfully. 'Takes a figure like mine to carry it off, of course, but Botty says I look like a queen in it.'

'Exactly, exactly,' said the young man, 'but I want yours to be the sort of programme that will *grip* the viewer, that will have *drama* and *realism* in it.'

'Dunno about drama,' said Mrs Bott doubtfully. 'I learnt a speech out of Shakespeare once when I was at school but I dunno if I could remember it. It was about a boy burnin' on a deck.'

'No, no,' said the young man. 'That wasn't Shakespeare, anyway. I mean the drama of everyday life. I want them to see a woman of beauty and culture like yourself' – again Mrs Bott smirked and bridled – 'coping with domestic upheavals. They'd remember that, when they've forgotten all the others. They'd see how you – left in the lurch like this without staff or domestic help – could still play the gracious hostess and handle the emergency with poise and humour and equanimity. It would give the programme the human touch that all the others have lacked.'

'D'you think so?' said Mrs Bott. She brightened. 'I could be scrubbin' the kitchen floor, couldn't I, with poise an' humour an' what you said? It's years since I scrubbed a kitchen floor with anythin'. I bet I could get it cleaner than them good-fer-nothin's.'

'No, no,' said the young man, shuddering slightly. 'Nothing of that sort. That must all be kept behind the scenes. You must just give me a humorous account of all the chores you've had to do in the course of the day now that you're left without staff.'

'You won't let 'em think we can't *afford* 'em, will you?' said Mrs Bott anxiously.

'No, no. We'll arrange it so that evidences of your – er – social and financial standing are very obvious. I'll have tea with you and you'll have made the cakes and scones yourself.'

'I'm not reely used to them electric cookers,' said Mrs Bott. 'I never seem to feel that they're reely *on* if they've not *popped* same as the gas ones used to.'

'Oh, of course you mustn't really make the cakes,' smiled the young man. I shouldn't dream of suggesting it. We'll buy them, of course, and there'll be no harm in your saying you've made them. A certain amount of poetic licence is always justified in such cases ... The first thing I must do is to get into touch with Lime Grove.'

'I could wear me pink,' said Mrs Bott thoughtfully, 'but I think me noo blue'd be better, don't you? No one's seen me noo blue an' I wore me pink at the Jumble Sale.'

'Splendid! Splendid! And I shouldn't tell anyone about it. We don't want a gaping crowd.'

'No,' agreed Mrs Bott. 'They can gape at it on their tellys, can't they, an' I bet they will, too, not 'arf! *H*arf.

'Exactly. Far better to tell no one at all. Let it burst on your friends as a surprise. It will go into a million homes, remember, and it will be a programme that will make history.'

'Fancy that!' said Mrs Bott, impressed.

'The gracious hostess coping with a staffless home ... I'll bring the television van along about three o'clock. Will that be all right?'

'Suit me a treat,' said Mrs Bott. 'But what about the programme that's printed in the telly paper?'

'Oh, we can easily adjust that,' said the young man

vaguely. 'We can introduce it as a surprise programme.'

'Yes, that's a good idea,' said Mrs Bott. 'Knock 'em into the middle of next week, won't it?'

'I'm quite sure it will . . . Let me see now. I don't even know your name.'

'Bott,' said Mrs Bott, 'an' I live at the Hall. You can't mistake it. Biggest 'ouse for miles round. *H*ouse. You could get that ole Steedham Grange inside our washin'-up machine. In a manner of speakin', of course. What's your name, by the way?'

'Call me Reggie,' said the young man with a pleasant smile. 'All my friends call me Reggie.'

'Nice name,' said Mrs Bott. 'We 'ad a bulldog called Reggie once. 'Oly terrer, 'e was, for peas. Couldn't stop eatin' 'em. Used to shell 'em all by 'isself.'

The young man laughed.

'Marvellous!' he said. 'But to return to this afternoon. I'll bring a colleague along to help with the equipment, of course.'

'I'll come and help with that,' said William.

They both turned round sharply, realising his presence in the car for the first time.

Reggie gave him an ugly scowl.

'What are you doing there?' he said.

'I got in when she did,' explained William.

'Always poking your nose in where it's not wanted William Brown,' said Mrs Bott.

'Well, I like *that*,' said William, stung by the injustice of the attack. 'It was me stopped the car, wasn't it? Gosh! I've a right to a lift, haven't I? An' – an' I can *help* with this television thing. I bet I'd be jolly good at doin' television. I bet—'

'WHAT ARE YOU DOING THERE?' ASKED REGGIE, GIVING WILLIAM AN
ANGRY SCOWL.

His voice died away. Reggie was watching him with
narrowed eyes. There was a look on his face that sent a
strange sinking feeling through William's stomach. But
when he spoke his voice was low and silky.

'Now listen! You are *not* coming to the Hall this afternoon. We don't need your help or your company. Kindly
understand that.'

'Yes, but—' began William, recovering his spirit.

Reggie interrupted.

'And kindly understand another thing. All this has to
be kept secret. Dead secret. If you breathe a word to

anyone of what you've heard in the car just now' – he smiled again but it was not a pleasant smile – 'something very horrible will happen to you.'

'What?' said William defiantly.

Reggie changed his tactics.

'Now listen!' he said. 'You look to me the sort of boy who can keep a secret. Well, this television interview is a secret between you and me and if you keep the secret and don't breathe a word of it to anyone, well – I'll see if I can find room for you later in some television show.'

'Gosh!' said William ecstatically. 'I'd like to be in a Cowboy one.'

'I dare say we could manage it,' said Reggie. His smile was still a little wolfish, but it was obviously meant to please. 'On condition, of course, that you don't breathe a word to anyone of what you've heard in the car about this television interview.'

'Course, I won't,' said William. 'Gosh! I can keep a secret.'

'It's most important that it should come on the viewers as a complete surprise.'

'Makin' hist'ry an' drama an' what not,' said Mrs Bott, complacently. 'And now shut up, William Brown. We've got more important thing to do than listenin' to your nonsense . . . Three o'clock . . . Well, I've got a lot to do if I'm to be a gracious hostess copin' with domestic up'eavals with poise an' so on by then. *H*eavels.' She frowned thoughtfully. 'I suppose I've not time to get a perm?'

'Hardly,' said Reggie, 'but' – he turned an admiring smile on the blonde curls that showed beneath Mrs Botts much-befeathered hat – 'it looks delightful as it is. Why gild the lily?'

'I wasn't thinkin' of gildin' no lilies,' said Mrs Bott. 'I 'aven't the time. I got a vase of sweet peas an' gypsophila in the drawing-room an' they'll 'ave to do.'

'Can I have a real cow to lassoo?' said William. 'I bet I could do one. I've tried on Jumble an' I nearly got him once.'

'Be quiet, William Brown!' snapped Mrs Bott. 'We've got more things to think of than cows. Here am I goin' into a million homes, makin' hist'ry an' drama, an' you've got to start on cows!'

Reggie looked round a little uneasily.

'Well, I think we might move on now. All you have to do, Mrs Bott, is to be ready to receive me and my colleague at three o'clock, and all *you* have to do' – his smile became a little wolfish again as he turned to William – 'is to keep your mouth shut.'

'I can do that all right,' said William airily.

'You promise?'

'Yes.'

Mrs Bott snorted and Reggie leant over to open the back door of the car.

'Out you get!' he said. 'You can walk to your home, wherever it is. Now I'll take you back to the Hall, Mrs Bott, and then see about collecting my colleague and equipment.' He pushed William out of the car with a final 'Remember what I said,' started up the car and disappeared down the main street of Hadley.

William stood and watched them out of sight, his mind a turmoil of emotion. He had touched the fringe of the magic world of television. He had met a real live television man. Already he saw himself on an imaginary screen, perched negligently on a bucking bronco, rounding up a herd of innumerable cattle with easy sweeps of his lassoo.

He thought over what the young man had said. He must keep the interview with Mrs Bott a secret. Well, he could do that all right. And he mustn't go near the Hall while the interview was taking place. That, he thought, was a mistake on the young man's part. The young man probably didn't realise how helpful he would be. Besides, he had his television career to think of. He must learn all he could about the working of television before his actual cowboy performance. Making his way home across the fields, giving spirited little jumps forwards, backwards and sideways, in response to the movements of his bucking bronco, he held the reins in one hand and with the other flung wide his lassoo over herds of imaginary cattle.

'Hi, there!' he shouted. 'Got you! Got You! *Got* you!'

His family was just sitting down to lunch when he arrived home. He took his seat with an impressive air of importance and secrecy, which failed, however, to impress his family.

'Go and wash your hands, William,' said Mrs Brown.

He tried to reproduce the young man's scowl as he rose from the table. Gosh, they'd treat him a bit diff'rent if they knew who he was. He went from the room with a scornful laugh and lassooed a dozen more cows on his way up to the bathroom.

He was finding his promise of secrecy rather hard to keep but he was determined to keep it.

'Huh!' he said as he took his seat at the table again. 'If you knew what I know.'

His family, who were accustomed to cryptic observations from William, betrayed neither interest nor curiosity.

'You might have brushed your hair while you were about it,' said Ethel.

'I wouldn't tell you even if you wanted to know,' said William, attacking his stew with wide sweeping movements as if rounding up yet another herd of wild cattle.

'Don't talk with your mouth full,' admonished Mrs Brown.

William finished his stew in silence and set to work on his apple tart.

'Huh!' he said, breaking his silence after the first mouthful, 'if you knew what's goin' to happen this afternoon only jus' – well, not a mile away, you'd be jolly s'prised.'

'Nothing you did would cause us any surprise, my son,' said Mr Brown unconcernedly.

'And don't fill your mouth so full, dear,' said Mrs Brown.

'And keep your elbows to yourself,' said Robert. 'You've nearly speared me once or twice already.'

'Your table manners are shocking,' said Ethel.

'Table manners!' echoed William in disgust. 'I bet *they* don't have 'em!'

'Who don't have what, dear?' said Mrs Brown.

'Cowboys,' said William. 'Table manners.' He swallowed the last mouthful of apple tart and rose from the table. 'Can I go now, please?'

'Yes,' said his family with sighs of relief.

He went out into the garden. Thoughts of his television career were giving way to thoughts of the momentous interview due to take place at the Hall this afternoon. He had been ordered to keep away but he hadn't promised to keep away and, right down at the bottom of his heart, he knew that he couldn't keep away.

He told himself that he would just take a little walk in the direction of the Hall. He took a little walk in the direction of the Hall. Finding himself at the gates of the Hall, he told himself that he would just take a little stroll up the drive. Just to make sure that everything was all right, that there would be nothing in the way when the young man arrived in his television van. He took a little stroll up the drive. There was nothing in the way. Finding himself outside the front door, he hesitated for a few seconds, then, on a sudden impulse, raised and dropped the heavy iron knocker.

Mrs Bott opened the door. She was in what her husband generally referred to as 'one of her states'. She couldn't get her hair right. She couldn't get her dress right. The staff, in their sudden unpremeditated departure, had left a track of 'downed tools' that seemed to catch her unawares whenever she moved. She'd already fallen over a pail of water and got entangled in the wires of an electric cleaner. She hadn't even started the preparations for tea. The 'home made' cake still reposed on the kitchen table in a carton that bore the name of a famous purveyor of confectionery.

'I jus' can't go on without 'elp,' she was moaning when William's knock summoned her to the front door.

William was not the help she would have chosen, but at the moment he seemed better than nothing.

'Come on in,' she snapped. 'Wipe your shoes an' come on in to the kitchen.'

Slightly bewildered, William followed her into the kitchen.

'Here's a tray,' she said tersely. 'Put two cups an' saucers on. Get the milk from the fridge. Get the sugar out. Get some plates. Take that cake out of the packet. Get the scones out of that bag. Find some jam from somewhere. Get some spoons. And get a move on, can't you?'

William got a move on. He broke a plate and dropped the butter. He upset the sugar and spilt the milk. Burrowing in the larder for some jam, he knocked a basin of gravy over on to Mrs Bott's shoes and followed it by a couple of new-laid eggs. Urged with increasing vehemence to 'find some jam from somewhere', he took a jam jar of soft soap from the window-sill and inspected it doubtfully.

'*Looks* like jam, anyway,' he said as he tipped it into an ornamental jam jar.

Mrs Bott scolded and harried and drove him. Even so, she did not altogether regret having asked him in. At least he was someone to scold and harry and drive.

Suddenly there came the sound of wheels outside . . . then a series of knocks on the front door.

'It's them,' panted Mrs Bott. 'Go an' open the door. I gotter clean myself up. All over butter an' milk an' egg an' gravy, I am, thanks to you, William Brown.'

William went to open the door. A van stood in the drive and on the doorstep stood Reggie, smiling genially, and another young man – a shifty-looking young man with small pig-like eyes, colourless eyelashes and a thin slit of a mouth.

The genial smile dropped from Reggie's face when he saw William.

'I didn't expect to find you here,' he said. He turned to the other young man. 'This is the boy I told you about, Len.'

'Pack him off,' said Len shortly.

'I don't know about that . . .' said Reggie slowly. 'After all, we've got him under our eyes here, haven't we? Perhaps it's safer.'

'Listen!' said William earnestly. 'I want to have a fight

with Red Indians, too. I want cows *an*' Red Indians.'

Then Mrs Bott appeared, still slightly dishevelled, but smiling with a radiance that made Reggie blink and step back a pace.

'*Sow* glad to see you, she said graciously. 'Come hin. Come hin.'

'How wonderful you look!' said Reggie as he entered.

'I've not 'ad time to do much titivatin',' said Mrs Bott. I've got a bottle of eye-shade somewhere, but I thought I'd better not put it on. I've only used it once an' Botty thought I'd got a couple of black eyes. I don't want to give them viewers a wrong impression.'

'Exactly, exactly,' said Reggie. He waved a hand at his companion. 'This is my colleague, Len.'

'*Sow* glad to see you,' said Mrs Bott. 'Wonderful weather we're 'avin the time o' year, aren't we? *H*avin'.'

'Now there isn't much time,' said Reggie, 'so we'd better set to work. I propose that you take us right over the house first, Mrs Bott, and show us the chief points of interest. Then we'll have our little tea-party and interview and after that do a round of the house so that the viewers can see the various rooms. Will that suit you?'

'Suit me a treat,' said Mrs Bott. 'I've got a gold an' tor- toiseshell set on me dressing-table. I'd like 'em to see that.'

'They shall,' said Reggie. 'Now lead the way.'

Mrs Bott led the way. She showed them the safe where her jewellery was kept and how it worked. She showed them where the silver was. She opened her wardrobe and showed them her mink coat, her ermine wrap and the hat with the diamond clip.

'That's splendid,' said Reggie. 'Now you and I will go downstairs and start the interview while my colleague here rearranges the upstairs rooms a little to make them more suitable for the camera. Then I suggest that you and I come upstairs again and take shots of all the rooms. There may possibly not be time for that part of the programme but we'll hope for the best. Do you agree?'

'Oh certainly,' said Mrs Bott. 'You won't forget me gold an' tortoiseshell set, will you?'

'No,' promised Reggie. 'We won't forget that.'

They went downstairs, leaving Len to his task.

'Now I'll get the tea' said Mrs Bott. 'Dunno 'ow long it'll take me. Them good-fer-nothin's 'ave left the place in such an uproar I can't make 'ead nor tail of it.'

'I'll help you,' said William, who had followed at the end of the procession, deeply interested in every detail of the arrangements.

'I've 'ad enough of your 'elp today to last me the rest of my life,' said Mrs Bott grimly, but she let William follow her into the kitchen and assist in the final preparations.

Things went a little better this time. William poured the water from the kettle to the tea-pot, with no further mishap than slightly scalding his own foot, and carried the tray into the drawing-room.

'All set for the interview!' said Reggie.

They looked at the 'equipment' with some surprise. It appeared to consist solely of a camera on a tripod stand.

'Where's the lights?' said William. 'I thought there'd be lights.'

'You're behind the times, young man,' said Reggie gaily. 'We don't use them any more.'

'Well, I must say, I thought there'd be a bit more machinery than this,' said Mrs Bott.

'I'll have to let you into a secret,' said Reggie. 'This is

my own invention. It supersedes the old-fashioned para-
phernalia of arc lamps, etc. The machinery, as you call it,
is actually all in the van.'

They looked out of the window and noticed a number
of small wires emerging from the closed door of the van,
crossing the drive, entering the window and vanishing
into the camera.

'Can you get all your machinery inside that there van?'
said Mrs Bott, wonderingly.

'Oh yes,' said Reggie. 'The van's chock-full of it, of
course. As I said, the thing's my own invention and it will
revolutionise the art of television. But just for the
moment I must ask you to keep it a secret. I'm in the process of patenting it, but of course there are certain unprin-
cipled people who are only too anxious to steal the secret.
I have to be very careful.'

'Gosh!' said William. 'S'pose someone's followed you
here?'

'That is a risk I have to take,' said Reggie.

'Is there anyone particular tryin' to steal it?' said
William, who liked every drama to have its own individ-
ual villain. 'I'll watch out for him if there is.'

'A good idea,' said Reggie.

'I bet he's a villain of the deepest dye who'll stick at
nothin' to get it,' said William earnestly.

'Exactly, exactly,' said Reggie, 'but we must get to
work . . . Now, Mrs Bott, take your place at the tea table
and begin to pour out the tea. Then we'll start the interview. I just switch on a small knob here inside the camera
and the thing begins to operate.'

'Well, wait a minute,' said Mrs Bott, settling herself in
her chair. 'Now you can start.'

'CAN YOU GET ALL YOUR MACHINERY IN THAT THERE VAN?' ASKED
MRS BOTT.

Reggie seated himself near the tea table.

'So delightful to see you in your charming home, Mrs Bott,' he said effusively.

' 'Ow, yes,' said Mrs Bott with a shattering smile. 'Sow naice of you to come! Do you taike sugah in your tea?'

'Yes, please . . . It must need a large staff to run a house of this size.'

'I'm runnin' it meself,' said Mrs Bott, forgetting her refinement as the bitter memories swept over her. 'Walked out on me, they 'ave, the set o' good-fer-nothin's!' She glanced at the camera. 'It's workin' all right, isn't it?'

'Oh, yes, recording every word and look.'

'Well 'ave a buttered scone an' some jam.'

Reggie glanced at the soft soap and shook his head.

'No, thank you.'

'A bit o' cake then,' she said, handing him the Swiss roll. ''Ome made, of course. *H*ome.'

'Really?' said Reggie. 'How splendid! Now how have you managed to provide me with this sumptuous tea without any staff?'

'Ow, no trouble at all!' said Mrs Bott with an airy gesture. 'I jus' flicked round with a duster an' knocked up a few cakes with – er – with poise an' so on. Nothin' to me at all. Stop larkin' about, William Brown.'

For William, trying to edge round the chair in which Mrs Bott was seated in order to get a better view of the camera, had tripped over a small footstool and fallen heavily against her.

'And in addition to all your other activities,' said Reggie suavely, 'you are kindly taking charge of a neighbour's child. A dear little chap!'

'Wot—'*im*?' said Mrs Bott, glaring at William. Then she recovered herself and bared her teeth again in the shattering smile. ' 'Ow yes, I'm hever so devoted to children, dear little innercents!'

Reggie made a short sharp gesture of dismissal in William's direction and William departed. He stood for a moment or two, irresolute, in the hall, then suddenly remembered the van. The precious machinery was there unguarded. The villain might have tracked it to the Hall and already made off with it. He was reassured by the sight of the van still standing in the drive. But suppose the precious machinery had been tampered with ... Cautiously he approached the van, opened the door, looked inside – and gave a gasp of horror. It was empty.

At least, it was empty of machinery. A suitcase of Mrs Bott's, which Len (now busy upstairs on the furs) had neatly packed with silver and jewellery, lay unobtrusively in a corner, but William hardly noticed that. The van had been 'chock-full of machinery'. There was now no machinery in it. The villain must have stolen a march on them, while they were engrossed in the 'interview', and made off with the whole invention. The ends of the wires lay on the floor of the empty van. Obviously they had been cut and the machinery removed.

He ran to the house and thrust his head through the open drawing-room window, interrupting Mrs Bott in an account of her lavish expenditure on the garden ('Chulips that big you'd 'ave thought they was cabbages if you 'adn't 'ave known they was chulips').

'He's been!' he gasped. 'It's gone!'

Mrs Bott turned to him, her features tensed in irritation. 'Go away, William Brown,' she said.

WILLIAM GAVE A GASP OF HORROR. THE VAN WAS EMPTY!

The young man also turned to William. He was nearing the end of his little adventure and couldn't afford to waste any time.

'Get out!' he said shortly.

William got out. They weren't going to listen to him, so he must do something on his own and do it quickly. His spirits rose as he came to the decision. Better, after all, that he should do it on his own. If he brought the villain to justice and saved the invention, the gratitude of the television authorities would know no bounds. They could hardly do less than feature him handsomely in his Cowboy and Indian programme. He'd have twenty cows. Fifty. A hundred. He'd conquer whole tribes of Red Indians single-handed. He'd ambush them, shoot them, lassoo them ... Then his mind returned to the present. The first thing to do was to find a clue and track down the villain.

He frowned thoughtfully at the van. A thief couldn't have slipped the whole vanful of machinery into his pocket. He must have had a van or a car to take it away in. He would begin by finding out in which direction it had gone. He went to the gate and examined the wheel tracks that led out to the road. There was one that looked smaller than the tracks that Reggie's van would have made. (Actually it was the milk cart, but William was not to know that.) He followed it for a few yards down the road then lost it and stood for a moment or two deliberating his next move.

As he stood there, he suddenly became aware of two men standing talking in the road near him. He recognised one as Mr Wakely, the Chief Constable. The other, who stood by a motor cycle from which he had evidently just dismounted, was a stranger.

'Odd running into you like this!' Mr Wakely was saying. 'Somehow one didn't expect to find the Yard here.'

The other man smiled.

'Oh, quite unofficial ... and probably a wild-goose chase. We traced this chap to this side of London and then lost sight of him. One or two clues seemed to lead in this direction, but I'm pretty sure now I'm on the wrong track, so I'm going back to London to start all over again.'

'What did you say he was? Burglar?'

'Well, his chief line is the confidence trick. He can get anything out of anyone. He got six hundred pounds out of a man in Brighton, four hundred pounds out of a man in Uxbridge, eighty pounds from an hotel-keeper in the New Forest, fifty pounds from a doctor in South London and another fifty from a clergyman in Essex. All in a few weeks. He's so plausible that he only has to lift a finger, it seems, and people thrust money at him. He can do a pretty neat job of ordinary burgling when put to it, but—'

'I know where he is!' burst out William breathlessly. ' 'Least, I know where he's been. He's jus' stolen a valu'ble television invention out of a television van. Jus' near here. I'll take you there an' I bet you find a clue.'

'Don't talk such nonsense, my boy,' said Mr Wakely severely, 'and don't listen to conversations that don't concern you. Go away.' He turned to the other man with a smile. 'I gather that the theft of inventions is hardly in your friend's line.'

The other man was looking thoughtfully at William.

'N-no,' he said. 'No, of course this chap wouldn't be interested in inventions, but I believe in exploring every avenue and leaving no stone unturned. There probably isn't anything in it but – come on then, young man. Take us to the scene of the crime.'

Pouring out eager explanations, William led them down the road to the gates of the Hall.

'You see, Mrs Bott was goin' on television, bein' a gracious hostess, an' this television man came along to do it an' he'd got a new television invention in his television van an' while he was doin' this television interview in the drawing-room this other man – this villain you're after – came along an' stole this television invention out of this television van an' I've found the marks of the car he took it away in an' then they sort of got muddled up with other marks but I'll take you to the van this invention was stolen out of an' I bet you'll find some clues, an' this television man'll be jolly grateful!'

They had reached the gate of the Hall now. The van was still in the drive. Reggie was just climbing up into the driving seat. There was rather a strained look on his face. Len had taken longer than he should have done over his part of the job. He had packed jewellery, silver and furs quickly enough, but had not been able to resist the temptation of making a somewhat prolonged tour of the house in order to add a few more valuables to his collection. He was now in the back of the van settling himself down among his suitcases. Mrs Bott was standing at the open window of the drawing-room. She was more flushed and dishevelled than ever but her face still wore its shattering smile.

'Goodbaie!' she called. 'Thank you hever so.'

The motor cyclist stood in the gateway taking in the scene.

'That's our man,' he said softly.

William had run up to the van, hailing Reggie with a loud shout.

'Hi! Listen! I've got someone to help you catch this thief. They're goin' to find clues an' I bet they get him. I—'

He stopped short.

Quite suddenly everybody seemed to be fighting everybody else, both on the driving seat and at the back

'I'VE GOT SOMEONE TO HELP YOU CATCH THE THIEF,'
SHOUTED WILLIAM.

of the car. There were shouts, bangs, piercing screams
from Mrs Bott, short sharp telephone messages, the
arrival of a police car ... then Reggie and Len, Reggie
still smiling and debonair, were removed from the scene.

It all happened so quickly that, thinking about it afterwards, William could never be quite sure what *had* happened.

But there was no doubt in the mind of Mrs Bott.

'If it 'adn't been for that there William Brown messin'
everything up,' she would say gloomily, 'I'd 'ave been on
the telly by now.'

Chapter 8

William and the Force of Habit

William sat gazing at the visitor, spellbound and fascinated.

The visitor was certainly an unusual sight. He had thick upstanding red hair, no eyebrows to speak of, small darting blue eyes, a long narrow mouth and a little tuft of carefully cultivated red hair on his chin.

He was the nephew of a friend of a friend of Mr Brown's, and the friend had written to Mr Brown to tell him that Cyprian Carruthers (the visitor's name) had taken a furnished cottage in the neighbourhood for a few weeks in order to write a book, and would Mr Brown be kind enough to look him up and take a neighbourly interest in him.

Mr Brown was kind enough. He wrote and asked Cyprian to tea. 'I don't know what we shall find to talk to him about,' Mrs Brown had said anxiously. But the first five minutes of Cyprian's visit dispelled her anxiety. One didn't have to find anything to talk to Cyprian about. Cyprian was quite prepared to do the talking himself without assistance from anyone. He talked without even

215

pausing for breath, and, as he talked, he seemed to gesticulate not only with his arms and head and hands and beard but with the whole of his thin wiry body. Occasionally his hand, flung out in an eloquent gesture, would hover for a second over the table of dainties prepared by Mrs Brown, swoop down on a biscuit, deposit it in the long thin mouth, then continue the interrupted gesture, while the flow of words never seemed to stop.

'The book that I'm writing,' he said, 'will give life a new meaning. It will revolutionise the whole human race. What is wrong with mankind at present is that it lets life *mould* it. Mankind must throw off the shackles of habit. Seize life. Grasp it. Mould it. Too long has mankind trod the well-worn paths in blinkers. Break the force of habit and life will become new each day. We're turning into sheep, into ants, into – well, into sheep and ants. Each one of us has the power of creating life afresh, of throwing off the shackles of habit' – he swooped up a small chocolate biscuit and flung it into his mouth as if feeding some imprisoned orator, then continued without a pause – 'and instead we spend our days working a treadmill. We bury our heads in the sand and hide from the glorious sunshine that fills the world.'

'Gosh!' said William faintly.

'If you really want to help anyone you love, break the force of habit in them,' continued Cyprian. 'Break the force of habit in them and let them start a new life.' He flung another biscuit to the imprisoned orator and went on, 'We might be supermen and potentates and we go about gagged and blinkered, blind and deaf and dumb.'

'Crumbs!' said William a little less faintly.

The visitor turned sharply to Mr Brown.

'What are you going to do tomorrow?' he said.

'Well – er—' said Mr Brown, recovering slowly from the paralysis that his visitor's eloquence had laid on him. 'Well – er – I shall go to the office and when I come home I shall mow the lawn.'

The visitor started forward in his chair and bent a piercing gaze on him.

'You always mow the lawn on Tuesdays?'

'Well, yes, I do.'

'*Don't*,' said Cyprian earnestly. 'Don't mow the lawn tomorrow. Claim your heritage as a free man and don't mow the lawn.'

'It'd get a bit shaggy,' said Mr Brown.

But his guest had turned to Mrs Brown.

'And you?' he demanded. 'What are you going to do tomorrow?'

'Oh . . . housework in the morning, I suppose,' said Mrs Brown, 'then the Women's Institute meeting in the afternoon and when I get home I shall set to work on the mending.'

'Do you always do the mending on Tuesdays?' said Cyprian, knitting his brows at her in a threatening fashion.

'Yes,' said Mrs Brown mildly. 'You see, by Tuesday evening the washing's dried and ironed and aired, and it seems the best day to set to work on the mending.'

The guest waved his arms like a disjointed windmill. His voice rose to a high squeaky note.

'Don't' he said. 'Make a start now, before it's too late. Tomorrow's Tuesday. Don't mow the lawn. Don't do the mending. Shake off your chains. Come out of your prison. Break the force of habit.'

A windmill-like gesture upset the sugar basin and, while they were picking up the pieces (assisted by William, who placed those he retrieved into his own mouth as the simplest way of disposing of them), Mrs Brown made a desperate effort to change the conversation.

'You're staying at Corner Cottage at Marleigh, aren't you?' she said.

'Yes,' said Cyprian, diving under the settee for a piece of sugar and placing it absent-mindedly in the jam jar.

'It belongs to the Fields, doesn't it?'

'Yes. They've gone abroad and let it to me,' said Cyprian.

'Have they taken their little girl with them? Agatha's her name, isn't it?'

'No, they haven't taken her,' said Cyprian. 'It seems they've parked her with an aunt who lives a few doors down the lane.' A far-away look came into his face and it settled into a complicated network of wrinkles as he added plaintively, 'A tiresome child.'

'The country's very pretty round there, isn't it?' said Mrs Brown, but she spoke without much hope. Already the gleam of fanaticism was returning to Cyprian's eye. Already he was extending his arms in a wild and sweeping gesture. Deftly Mrs Brown moved the milk jug out of his range.

'I am a man with a mission,' he said. 'A mission to mankind. Why has joy left the human race? Because habit had been enthroned in its place.' He shot his head forward, fixing his piercing gaze again on host and hostess. 'Why do *you* look so bored and despondent?' Mr and Mrs Brown tried hastily to banish the looks of boredom and despondency from their faces. 'Because you are the slaves of custom, the prisoners of habit, the—'

The hall clock struck five, and Cyprian leapt to his feet.

'I'm afraid I must be going. I like to start my evening session of work at five-thirty and it takes me some little time to compose my thoughts. Thank you for a delightful visit. I'll let you know when my book comes out. It will take the world by storm. It will sweep through it like a forest fire. There will be opposition, of course – groans, boos, gnashings of teeth—' He stopped short, startled by the crunching of a piece of sugar on which he had inadvertently placed his foot. 'Well, once again, good-bye, good-bye, good-bye.'

Mr Brown saw him to the gate. When he returned Mrs Brown was lying relaxed in the chair with closed eyes and William, released from the spell by the departure of the visitor, was making up for lost time and demolishing the remains of the tea. Mr Brown sank into his own chair, took out his handkerchief and mopped his brow.

'That young man's first visit here,' he said fervently, 'shall be his last. I hope never to set eyes on him again.'

'It wasn't eyes so much as ears,' said Mrs Brown. 'I can still hear him, can't you? It was simply shattering.'

'It was more than that,' said Mr Brown. He gave a chuckle. 'There's something in it, of course. I've no doubt it would do us all the good in the world to get out of our ruts, but it would take more will-power than I possess to do it.'

'And I don't think I want to get out of my rut,' said Mrs Brown.

'I don't either,' said Mr Brown. 'I suppose that's the worst of it.'

He turned to look at his son with an expression of wonder. William was still busy with the remains of the tea. He held a scone in one hand and a piece of iced cake in the other.

'I don't think I've ever known you so quiet for so long, my boy,' he said.

'Well, I was *listenin'*,' said William indistinctly. 'Gosh! He was talkin' so much there wasn't anythin' you could do *but* listen. He said some jolly int'restin' things, too. An' he could talk an' eat an' talk an' eat on an' on an' on all at the same time.'

'You're not too bad at that yourself,' said Mr Brown, adding in mechanical reproof, 'Don't talk with your mouth full.'

'It's not full,' said William. 'It'll hold a lot more than what it's got in it now. Why, once it held—'

'Well, don't eat any more now,' interrupted Mrs Brown. 'You've had quite enough.' She rose from her chair. 'And I suppose I'd better get to work on the tea things.'

'Shall I help you wash up?' said William.

'No, thank you dear,' said Mrs Brown quickly and a little apprehensively, adding on a rather forced note of gratitude, 'It's very kind of you, dear, but I think it would do you good to get out into the fresh air.'

'I'll go an' see how Ginger is, then,' said William.

Ginger was confined to the house with a mild attack of measles and William paid him visits at regular intervals to note the progress of his rash.

'Wash your face first,' said Mrs Brown.

As the door closed on him William heard his mother say, 'It does seem funny without Robert and Ethel, doesn't it?'

* * *

To William, too, it seemed funny without Robert and Ethel. It seldom happened that Robert and Ethel were away from home at the same time. Ethel was staying with an old school friend in Lincolnshire and Robert was helping Jameson Jameson with a boys' camp on the south coast. When William first heard of these arrangements his spirits had risen. The prospect of home life without an elder brother and sister to snub him and order him about was an exhilarating one. But, oddly, when it came it turned out to be disappointingly flat. He found that he missed the snubs and ordering about; missed, most of all, the state of warfare that generally existed between himself on one side and Robert and Ethel on the other. Life seemed dull and uneventful without it.

Moreover, to make matters worse, Robert and Ethel had held a sort of ceremonial conference with him before they left, exacting a solemn promise from him to be good and help his mother and father as much as he could during their absence. William had taken the promise seriously and had 'helped' assiduously and on the whole, he considered, successfully. His washing-up had resulted in the demolition of only two cups, one saucer and an already cracked cake plate. He had carried in the coke, and the bucket he had upset had left only a few traces on the kitchen carpet. He had gone on a shopping expedition, lost his shopping list, and by a supreme effort of memory had brought home an ounce of sugar and two pounds of pepper.

But he was becoming bored by the situation. There was no excitement in it, and William liked any situation with which he was concerned to have a little excitement in it.

He trudged along the road to Ginger's, his hands thrust into his pockets, his brow drawn into a frown. Surely there were ways of 'helping' that held a little more adventure than washing-up and getting in coke. Then gradually – very gradually – a light seemed to break through his gloomy countenance. He remembered the visitor's words, 'If you really want to help anyone you love, break the force of habit in them.' Cyprian Carruthers had urged Mr Brown to refrain from mowing the lawn tomorrow. He had urged Mrs Brown to refrain from doing her household mending. They had agreed that it might be a good thing if they followed his advice.

'I've no doubt that it would do us all the good in the world to get out of our ruts,' his father had said, 'but it would take more will-power than I possess to do it.'

Well, he William, would supply the will-power. He would help them out of their ruts. It would be keeping his promise to Robert and Ethel and it would introduce a little much-needed adventure into life. His drooping figure straightened itself. His brow cleared. In a sudden burst of exuberance he took a running leap at a five-barred gate, performed a 'vault' that landed him head first on the other side, picked himself up, vaulted back again into the road, fell into the ditch, picked himself up again, brushed himself down in a hasty and perfunctory manner and set off at a run across the fields to Ginger's house.

Having arrived there he took up a small stone and threw it at Ginger's bedroom window. After a short interval Ginger appeared.

William inspected him critically.

'Gosh! There's hardly any left,' he said.

He spoke in the aggrieved tone of one who has been

defrauded of his rights. He had come to take an almost proprietary interest in Ginger's spots.

'Well, I can't help it,' said Ginger. 'They go. They go by themselves. It's their nature. I bet there won't be any left by tomorrow. Anyway,' with a sudden burst of spirit, 'they're *my* spots, aren't they?'

'I s'pose so,' said William grudgingly. 'But you can't see them, so it doesn't matter to you whether they go or stay. They've been jolly int'restin' to watch. They were *smashin'* the day before yesterday.'

'Well, I'm sick of 'em,' said Ginger. 'You can have the whole lot of 'em for all I care. I'll be jolly glad when it's over an' I can go out an' do somethin' int'restin'. What are you goin' to do tomorrow?'

'I'm goin' to do somethin' jolly excitin' tomorrow,' said William.

'What?' persisted Ginger.

'I'll tell you,' said William slowly and portentously. 'I'm goin' to break the force of habit.'

Ginger considered this for a moment or two in silence.

'Break the what?' he said at last.

'The force of habit,' said William. 'I'm goin' to start with my father an' mother an' then I'll prob'ly go on to other people. I'm goin' to join in this mission for breakin' the force of habit an' gettin' people out of their ruts. A man was talkin' about it at our house an' he writes books so he mus' know.'

'Well, how are you goin' to start?' said Ginger.

'I'm goin' to start on mendin' an' mowin',' said William, 'I'm—'

The kitchen door opened and Ginger's mother appeared. She dismissed William unceremoniously. William, who was accustomed to being dismissed unceremoniously by his friends' parents, took his departure without protest.

'Tell me about it when you've done it,' pleaded Ginger, leaning out of his bedroom window.'

'All right,' said William, going towards the gate. 'It's goin' to give 'em a new life an' rev'lutionise the whole human race.'

'Gosh!' said Ginger. 'When are you goin' to start?'

'Tomorrow,' called William from the road. 'The thinkin' out'll prob'ly take till then.'

But the 'thinking out' seemed unexpectedly easy. All he had to do was to hide his father's mowing machine and his mother's bag of mending. They would come home, search for them in vain, then perforce they would have to find something else to do. The force of habit would have been broken. They would have been thrown out of their rut. The first, the hardest, step would have been taken. They could start on their new lives.

The next day his mother got ready for her Women's Institute meeting immediately after lunch.

'Aren't you going out, dear?' she said as she opened the front door.

'Soon,' said William. 'I'm goin' out soon.'

A note of subdued excitement in his voice should have warned Mrs Brown that something was afoot, but she had been deputed to introduce the visiting speaker, who was to address the gathering on 'Calories and Diet', and her mind was so busy trying to frame a few suitable words and to remember exactly what calories were that she had no attention to spare for subtle shades of voice or manner in her young son.

'Well, mind you shut the door when you go,' she said

absently as she walked down the path, her lips silently forming the words, 'We are all of us, of course, familiar with the meaning of the term "calories".'

William wasted no time. The mowing machine first of all . . . He went down to the garden shed and gazed at it with a thoughtful frown. It was not a large mowing machine because the Browns' lawn was not a large lawn, but even a small mowing machine is a difficult thing to hide. Impossible to conceal it behind a bag of rose fertiliser or even behind the rhododendron that was the largest bush the Brown garden boasted. William had had the idea of taking it up to Robert's bedroom and hiding it under the bed, but a few moment's reflection told him that the operation would be difficult if not impossible. Grasping the handles, he wheeled it out of the shed, round the house and down the path to the front gate.

Between the road and the hedge that surrounded the garden ran a dry ditch, deep and wide enough to form a convenient hiding-place. Lowering the machine into it was a more difficult operation than William had foreseen. At first it refused even to approach the ditch, then, suddenly changing its mind, took a wild leap into it, dragging William behind. He extricated himself as best he could and climbed out, his knees cut, his forehead bruised, his person sprinkled with soil and twigs, and surveyed the scene critically. Yes, it was all right. No sign of the mowing machine could be seen from the road.

There remained his mother's bag of household mending. He went to the cupboard under the stairs, where it hung from a rail, bulging with socks and shirts, pillow slips and pyjamas. High up at the back of the cupboard ran a long shelf, containing household stores packed in cardboard boxes. He took down the bag of mending and thrust it on to the shelf behind the cardboard boxes with no greater casualty than the descent of a bottle of turpentine on his head. Yes, you couldn't see it there. It was quite hidden. They'll be out of their ruts, all right, he thought complacently, and they can start their new lives straight away.

He stood there, considering his next step. Some instinct urged him to remove himself as far as possible from the scene of his activities. So apt were his parents to connect any disorganisation of the household with his presence that he felt the breaking of the force of habit would stand a better chance to work quickly and effectively if he were not there.

Moreover, ever since Cyprian's visit he had felt a deep and consuming interest in the writer himself. He decided to make his way over to Marleigh, inspect the outside of the cottage and, perhaps, catch a glimpse of the 'man with the mission' at his ennobling work.

Hands in pockets, whistling untunefully, he set off again over the fields. At the back of his mind a faint – a very faint – feeling of apprehension was gathering. Well, I did it for their *good*, he assured himself. He said it would be a mental tonic. Well, I've given 'em a mental tonic, haven't I? Gosh! People pay *money* for tonics an' I've given 'em one free. They ought to be jolly grateful to me. They'll turn into supermen an' potentates. He tried to imagine his parents as supermen and potentates but found it difficult. It was easier to imagine himself as superman and potentate.

He became a superman and potentate. Swaggering down the hill, he moved vast armies by a wave of his grubby hand. Conquered rulers trembled at a flicker of his soil-encrusted brow. A delegation of inhabitants of the Moon waited patiently to proffer their allegiance. The greatest scientists of the world were fashioning secret weapons for him. He thrust aside the crown that loyal hands were trying to press on his dishevelled head. 'No,' he said sternly, 'I'm a soldier an' I've not quite finished conquerin' the world. There's still whole countries to be ground under my heel before I set up to be king . . . Follow me, men.'

Waving an imaginary sword, he led his vast horde of warriors down the hill and along the narrow lane at the bottom.

Then he stopped short, for he found himself passing Corner Cottage.

It was a small, pretty cottage at the junction of the lane and a quiet country road. A little girl stood at the side gate. She carried a dilapidated gollywog in one hand and a basket in the other.

'Hello,' said William, dismissing his warriors and stopping being a potentate.

She scowled at him.

'Hello,' she said. 'What's your name?'

'William. What's yours?'

'Agatha.'

William's eyes wandered to the cottage.

'That's where that man lives that writes about breakin' the force of habit,' he said.

The look of sulkiness on the little girl's face intensified to one of fury.

'He's a robber,' she said. 'He's a robber and a thief and a burglar.'

'Gosh! I didn't know about that,' said William startled. 'I thought he was jus' a writer about gettin' people out of their ruts an' breakin' the force of habit.'

'No, he's a *stealer*,' said the little girl vehemently.

'What does he steal?' said William with interest.

'Houses,' said the little girl. She pointed dramatically to the cottage. 'That's *my* house an' he's stolen it. It *belongs* to me. I've lived there all my life and now he's stolen it. He's sitting on our chairs and sleeping in our beds and having baths in our bath and cooking kippers on our gas cooker and – and – and he's a wicked man and he ought to be in prison.'

William considered the situation thoughtfully.

'Yes, but he told us about it when he came to tea. He's rented it. He's payin' your father and mother money for it while they're away.'

The little girl waved the explanation aside impatiently.

'That's nothing to do with it. He's taken our house and he's a robber and a thief and a burglar. I keep on and on coming to try to stop him using our things and he jus' sends me away.'

'Yes, but—' began William.

'Yesterday he was drinking tea out of my mug – *my* mug with pussy on it – and the day before he was using my potato peeler to peel his potatoes – the little one that Mummy always lets me keep for myself – and when I tried to stop him he wouldn't listen and just sent me away.'

'When are your father and mother coming back?' said William.

'Next week.'

'Well, it'll soon be next week,' said William, vaguely reassuring.

The little girl stamped her foot angrily.

'Don't be so silly,' she said. 'It's today that's important.'

'Why?'

'It's his birthday.'

'Whose?'

'*His*,' she said, jerking up the dilapidated gollywog. 'Don't be so stupid. It's *his* birthday. Sambo's. It's his birthday and every birthday since he was born he's had a birthday picnic in the little summer-house in the front garden. I've got the things in my basket all ready for it, but that horrible man's sitting writing at the front window – it's *our* window, he's stolen that, too – and he can see the summer-house and he won't let me go into it.'

Again William considered the situation. It was a situation that seemed to hold an infinite number of possibilities, and situations of that sort always appealed to William.

'Well,' he began at last, but the little girl interrupted him, her eyes bright with anger.

'I came and waited here 'cause I thought a *p'liceman* might come along or some big strong man that could help me. I didn't know that only a silly little boy would come.'

William stared at her, dumbfounded.

'*Me?*' he said. '*Me?* A silly little boy? Gosh! I've conquered half the world, I've got hundreds of armies at my beck an' call. I've trod where the foot of man has never trod before. I've swept whole continents like a ragin' torrent. I've got generals an' admirals an' – an'

'ME A SILLY LITTLE BOY?' SAID WILLIAM. 'GOSH I'VE CONQUERED
HALF THE WORLD.'

schoolmasters hangin' on my words. I've got secret
weapons that make this H-bomb look jus' silly. I've got
people off the Moon beggin' me to be their Mayor.
I've—'

He paused for breath. The little girl was looking at him, impressed but not wholly convinced.

'Then surely you can do a little thing like giving Sambo his birthday picnic.'

'Well, that's a bit diff'rent,' said William.

'If you can't do anything,' said the little girl, 'go away. I'm tired of you.'

But William didn't want to go away. The situation had him in its grip.

'Let's go an' have a look at it from the front,' he said.

The little girl followed him round to the front of the cottage and the two peered through the hedge at the tumbledown summer-house that stood in a corner of the garden, then at the rose-encircled window where the author sat writing, his head bent over his writing desk. Occasionally he raised his head and flashed a suspicious glance round the garden.

'He looks up like that whenever I try to go in,' said the little girl plaintively, 'and then he comes out and sends me away. He gets wickeder and wickeder every minute. He ate one of our lettuces yesterday. I saw him doing it. *Eating* it! *Our* lettuce. Just as if it belonged to him. And this morning he had an egg in the little egg cup that Father Christmas gave me. It had my *name* on, too. He's so wicked, he ought to have his head chopped off.

William was busy studying the lie of the land.

'He couldn't see you once you were right *inside* the summer-house,' he said.

'I know that, silly!' snapped the little girl, 'but he sees me goin' there an' stops me. And poor Sambo can't have his picnic and you won't do anything about it and you don't even *care*.'

There was a hint of tears in her voice.

'Yes, I do,' protested William. 'Honest, I do. I'm tryin' to think of a way.' He stood frowning sombrely, then gradually his brow cleared. 'Gosh! I've got it! I've got an idea. Now listen!'

'Yes?'

'I'll go round to the other door an' keep him talking an' while he's talking you can slip into the summer-house an' by the time he's got back to his desk you'll be right inside the summer-house an' he can't see you. That's a jolly good idea, isn't it?'

The little girl pursed her lips.

'Um-m-m. Well, it *might* be,' she said non-committally.

'It jolly well *is*,' said William. 'It's smashin'. Now let's start. You get ready at the front door an' I'll go to the other one.'

They separated. The little girl made her way round to the front gate and William entered the side gate and beat a loud tattoo on the green door. It was opened by Cyprian, a fountain-pen poised in one hand. The small blue eyes fixed themselves on William in irritated query. He did not recognise William. He knew, of course, that there had been a boy at the Browns' house on his visit there, but to Cyprian all boys were alike – undersized creatures with grubby faces and tousled hair.

'What do you want?' he said shortly.

''Scuse me,' said William in a tone of exaggerated politeness, 'but does Mr Robinson live here?'

'No,' said Cyprian, slamming the door and vanishing.

William went round to the corner of the road. The little girl was approaching it.

'That wasn't any good at all,' she said indignantly. 'He was back before I'd got through the gate.'

'Yes, I'm sorry,' said William. 'I'd got some jolly int'restin' things to talk to him about, but he wouldn't listen. I'll try again. Go back to the gate an' wait.'

Again he beat the long and challenging tattoo on the side door. Again the face of Cyprian, tensed in exasperation, appeared in the aperture.

Cyprian, of course, could have ignored William's attack on his door, but it happened that he had written to a firm of publishers yesterday, sending a synopsis of his book and hinting that innumerable other publishers were interested and that an immediate reply was necessary to secure it for their list. With the optimism of the creative artist he had been expecting a telegram all day.

'What do you want now?' he snapped.

''Scuse me,' said William with an oily smile, 'but could you kin'ly tell me the time?'

'No,' snarled Cyprian, slamming the door again.

William went to the corner of the road. The little girl's expression was almost as forbidding as Cyprian's had been.

'You are a *stupid* boy,' she said. 'I hadn't got inside the gate when he came back that time.'

'Well, I tried,' said William. 'I'd thought up a lot more things to say to him – jolly int'restin' ones, too – to keep him talkin', but he wouldn't let me start. Listen! You go back an' I'll try again. I've thought of somethin' jolly int'restin' this time.'

He returned once more to the side door and beat the knocker.

The door opened a few inches and the anxious inquiring face of Cyprian showed itself once more.

'Can I have a drink of water, please?' said William, then remembering the expression that his mother's daily help had used yesterday, added, 'I've come over queer.'

'You've *what?*' almost screamed Cyprian.

'Come over queer,' said William, fixing him with a stony glare as he insinuated his solid figure through the doorway.

Nonplussed, uttering little chirps of irritation, Cyprian filled a mug at the kitchen tap and handed it to William. William sipped it in a slow and leisurely fashion, surveying the kitchen as he did so.

'It's a nice kitchen,' he said in a pleasant conversational tone of voice. 'I should think it'd be a jolly good kitchen for workin' in – better than that ole front room. It's got a jolly good table to work at an'—'

He stopped short. Cyprian had snatched the mug from his hands and with unexpected dexterity slung him on to the doorstep, slamming the door. William picked himself up and stood for a moment, sternly admonishing the closed door.

'Gosh! Some people've got some jolly funny manners! A visitor comes over queer an' all he gets is bein' sprung at an' thrown about.'

But the whole process had taken some little time and it was in a more hopeful frame of mind that he set off to the corner of the road. He was dismayed to find the little girl waiting for him, her small face set again in lines of fury.

'But gosh!' said William. 'I gave you some time then. I – I had a drink with him. I had a little talk with him. Gosh! I gave you a *lot* of time.'

'Well, it wasn't enough,' said the little girl. 'It wasn't half enough. I dropped the basket when I was going through the gate and everything fell out of it and by the time I'd picked them up he was back again at the window. You aren't any good at all. And I'm so unhappy.' Again the threat of tears invaded her voice. 'All his life Sambo's had a picnic in the summer-house on his birthday and now, just because you won't take just a bit of trouble—'

CYPRIAN SLUNG WILLIAM ON TO THE DOORSTEP.

'I *am* takin' trouble,' expostulated William. 'I'm jus' about worn out with all the trouble I'm takin'. Listen! I'll have another try. I'll have another try now. I bet I can keep him talkin' all right this time.'

He went down the lane and began his resounding attack on the door again.

The author, seated at his desk once more, shuddered, groaned and dropped his head into his hands. That wretched boy again! But – just possibly it mightn't be that wretched boy again. Just possibly it might be the bearer of a telegram from the post office. 'Your splendid book accepted. Contract following.' Reluctantly, still shuddering, he rose from his seat and went to the door.

So anxious had William been to redeem his failure and engage Cyprian in a lengthy conversation that he had omitted to prepare an opening gambit. As the familiar face of the writer, twisted into a grimace of anguish, appeared in the doorway, he tried desperately hard to think of one. And suddenly inspiration answered his call. He had read a story last week in which the hero had gained admission to a gloomy castle in order to foil the sinister machinations that were taking place within. Without stopping to consider whether they were appropriate to the occasion, he used the words with which the hero had addressed the ancient servitor who opened the castle door. His eyes were glassy, his face expressionless as he repeated them.

'May I shelter from the storm here, my good man?'

The distracted author gave a strangled scream of rage and flung himself on William with the fury of despair. William dodged, slipped and fell, picked himself up and once more found himself standing outside a closed door. Slowly he rejoined the little girl at the corner of the road.

'Yes, I know,' he said, forestalling her reproaches. 'Yes, I know . . . He won't listen to me. He's got a guilty conscience. He's frightened of talkin' to me 'cause of this guilty conscience. I could tell he was scared of me, the way he looked at me. He's afraid I'm goin' to bring him to justice. Well, stands to reason he is. He wouldn't even let me shelter from the storm. He's got somethin' to hide, all right, that's why he's been tryin' to get out of talkin' to me. Gosh! You should've seen him this las' time. He was shakin' all over with guilt.'

'What storm?' said the little girl, half sceptical, half impressed.

William looked up at the cloudless sky.

'Well, there's always storms about,' he said vaguely. 'They come up sudden. It might start thunderin' or hailin' any minute an' nat'rally I wanted to take shelter before it started.'

But the little girl had returned to her grievances.

'Sambo's never had such a miserable birthday in all his life,' she said. 'You keep him hanging round and hanging round . . . You pretend you can do things and you can't do anything. I wish you'd never come here. I wish I'd never met you. I wish—'

'Stop *talking* and tell me what it is,' said the little girl.

'It's a smashing idea,' said William, loath to leave the subject of his own cleverness. 'I bet no one but me could have thought of it. I bet—'

'Tell me what it is and stop *talking*,' said the little girl again impatiently.

'All right,' said William solemnly. 'I'll tell you. I'm goin' to smoke him out.'

She stared at him.

'*What?*' she said.

'Smoke him out,' repeated William. 'My mother had a letter from someone last week an' they said they'd been smoked out of their sitting-room 'cause there was a bird's nest in the chimney. Well, I'm goin' to put a bird's nest in his chimney an' smoke him out so's he can't work in that front room an' he'll have to go an' work in the kitchen –

there's a jolly good table for workin' at in the kitchen. I told him so but he wouldn't listen – an' then you can go into the summer-house for your picnic an' he won't see you.'

The little girl considered the plan with pursed lips.

'It might be all right,' she said at last.

''Course it'll be all right,' said William. 'It couldn't go wrong. Now let's get started. You go round to the front again an' keep an eye on him. I don't want him to find me doin' it. He'd get mad again 'cause of this guilty conscience he's got. If he goes away from the window, come an' tell me so's I can keep out of his way. Anyway, I won't be long. Jus' a bird's nest an' it looks a jolly easy climb to the roof.'

He made his way round to the little garden at the back of the cottage and began a hasty and unsuccessful search for a bird's nest.

'Gosh!' he muttered aggrievedly as he peered into hedges and bushes. 'Don't they want to *live* anywhere? Don't they want any *homes?* Can't they even bother to *build* 'em any more? Gosh, it's not all that trouble puttin' a few sticks an' bits of grass together. Why, I could have done it myself, the time I've been looking . . .'

That suggested an idea to him. Picking up some twigs from under the hedge and a few handfuls of grass from the overgrown lawn, he rammed them together into a ball, thrust them into his pocket and turned to consider the structure of the cottage. A pipe ran from a rain tub to the gutter on the roof. If he stood on the rain tub, it was only a short distance to the roof. He stood on the rain tub, one foot on each side, then took hold of the pipe to swing himself up, wobbled uncertainly and slipped into the rain tub. There had been no rain for several weeks and the rain tub was only quarter full, but it had not been cleared out for several years and a thick coating of green slime covered William's legs when he emerged from it.

Once launched on his climb, however, he found the ascent fairly easy. Metal strips secured the pipe to the wall and gave him good foothold. He rested for a moment on the gutter to survey the sloping roof that led to the chimney, then set out on the last stage of his journey. Reaching the chimney, he stood upright and peered down the aperture, feeling in his pocket for his improvised bird's nest.

And then – the unexpected happened.

Cyprian had, in a frenzy of inspiration, finished the third chapter of his book. Gathering together the mass of notes from which he had been working, he flung them on the fire. The flames sprang up. The smoke bellied out of the chimney, catching William full in the face, blinding, choking, blackening him. Sputtering and coughing, he clawed the air for a few seconds, then lost his balance and slid down the roof, clutched at the gutter, missed it, clutched at the climbing rose that covered the cottage and descended with it on to the little lawn in the front garden.

Cyprian darted out of the cottage. The little girl came running in at the gate.

They stood staring at the weird object before them – black-faced, green-legged, entwined in climbing roses.

Cyprian flung his arms heavenwards.

'The boy! The wretched boy!' he screamed. He shook a thin quivering fist in William's face. 'You've ruined my working day. Here am I writing a book that's going to destroy the force of habit and free mankind from its

WILLIAM LOST HIS BALANCE AND SLID DOWN THE ROOF.

shackles and you break into my working hours and ruin my whole day's time-table.'

'And he's spoilt Sambo's birthday,' put in the little girl

tearfully. 'He's a horrible boy. I wish he'd never come here.'

William swallowed a mouthful of soot and removed a piece of climbing rose from the back of his neck.

'Yes, but listen—' he began.

'I'm at the most important stage of my work,' said Cyprian. 'The next chapter is *crucial*! And here you come, banging at the door, barging down off the roof, tearing down the vegetation, laying waste the whole property. If I weren't expecting an important telegram, I wouldn't have answered the door at all, but how was I to know that each time you knocked it wasn't someone from the post office with an important telegram, bringing me a vital piece of news?'

The little girl was gazing at Cyprian. Her eyes were large and innocent, her expression angelic.

'I think I could help you, Mr Carruthers,' she said sweetly.

Cyprian turned to her.

'You?' he said incredulously.

Despite the incredulity there was hope and appeal in his voice. He had looked on her as a disturber of his peace, a shatterer of his privacy, but that was before he had known William.

She fluttered her eyelashes and gave him a ravishing smile.

'Yes, Mr Carruthers,' she said. 'If I sit in the summer-house in that corner of the garden, I can see anyone who comes to the other door and I can tell you whether it's a telegraph boy or this awful boy again.'

Cyprian drew a deep breath.

'Oh, that would be kind of you,' he said gratefully. 'I wish you would.'

'Yes, but—' began William.

'Go away!' said Cyprian.

The little girl raised her head and turned it to one side, wrinkling up her nose in a grimace eloquent of disgust and revulsion.

'Yes, please go away,' she said. 'I never want to see you again as long as I live.'

'All right,' said William coldly as he disentangled himself from a length of trailing rose tree. 'I don't want to stay where I'm not wanted. I've—'

A plunging movement of Cyprian's in his direction hastened his steps to the gate and he walked down the road with as much dignity as he could command. Gosh, he muttered, thrusting his hands deep into his pockets, all that trouble an' not even a word of thanks! Riskin' my life for her in rain tubs an' chimneys an' she can't even say 'thank you'. I tried to get her ole picnic for her. Gosh! I *did* get it, too. If it hadn't been for me he'd never have let her have her ole picnic in the summer-house at all.

He stopped in his tracks, wondering whether to go back and point this out, then decided not to. He removed a few more pieces of trailing rose bush from his person, tried ineffectually to brush some of the green slime from his stockings, then trudged on down the road, sending his mind back over the afternoon's events. He had set out to break the force of habit and had been deflected from his purpose by the little girl's problem. But at least there remained his father and mother. In their case, at any rate, he must have succeeded. His father could not have mown the lawn. His mother could not have done her mending. He would have broken the force of habit in them and they could now start their new lives.

Aware that this afternoon's activities must have left their traces on his person, he entered the house soundlessly, crept upstairs to his bedroom and set to work to remove as much of the mess as he could. He changed his stockings, washed the green off his legs, then turned to consider his face. Its reflection interested him so deeply that it was some time before he could bring himself to begin the task of restoring it to its original colour; but at last, cleaned and tidied in a sketchy fashion, he went down to the sitting-room.

His father sat in an armchair, reading the evening paper. His mother was turning over the pages of a magazine. William studied them, searching for traces of the new life on which they must now have started.

His father looked up from his paper.

'Sensible of you to put out the mowing machine, my boy,' he said.

William stared at him.

'Put out—?'

'The mowing machine. It completely slipped my mind that I'd told Erskine I'd put it out near the gate for him to collect.' He smiled. 'You needn't have put it right in the ditch, of course, but I see why you did it. There's a lot of pilfering going on these days and you left it nicely hidden. Actually Erskine found that it only needed a new chain and he fixed one on and was bringing it back again as I came home.'

William blinked and gulped and swallowed.

'You mean you – you mowed the lawn same as usual?'

'Of course, my boy.'

'Oh, and it was thoughtful of you to move the mending bag, too, William,' said Mrs Brown.

William moistened his lips.

'Move the—'

'The mending bag, dear. I hadn't noticed that the pipe just above it was leaking. Just at the join, as I suppose you noticed, and just above the bag. Only a few drips every now and then, but it would have made a nasty mess of things. The plumber was passing as I came in and he soon fixed it for me.'

'You – you found the bag?' said William hoarsely.

'Yes, dear, of course I did. As I say, it was very thoughtful of you to move it from under the dripping pipe and put it on the shelf.'

'An' you did your mendin' same as usual?'

'Yes, of course, dear. I always do on Tuesdays.' She looked more closely at her son and gave a cry of horror. 'William, you look dreadful. What *have* you been doing?'

'Nothin',' said William. 'I mean, nothin' much. I mean, jus' a few little things. I mean—'

'Your face is *black*! And *look* at your knees! And what on earth are all those leaves and things sticking all over you?'

'Oh, jus' soot an' water an' bits of tree,' said William, edging towards the door. 'Well, I'll go'n' see how Ginger's gettin' on.'

'But, William—'

William had vanished. He was making his way over the field to Ginger's. Gosh! All that trouble for nothin', he was thinking. Oh, well, he'd done his best. He couldn't do anything more. They'd just have to go on like sheep and ants in blinkers, working a treadmill with their heads buried in the sand.

Ginger appeared at the window in answer to his summons.

'I'm afraid a good many more have gone since yesterday,' he said apologetically.

'Oh, well,' said William gloomily. 'I s'pose it's same as everythin' else. It jus' can't be helped.'

'How did you get on?' said Ginger. 'Did you get anyone out of their ruts?'

'No,' said William morosely. Then his mind went again over the events of the afternoon and he brightened. 'Yes, I did. I got myself out of mine.'